BEST SELLER ROMANCE

A chance to read and collect some of the best-loved novels from Mills & Boon—the world's largest publisher of romantic fiction.

Every month, four titles by favourite Mills & Boon authors will be re-published in the *Best Seller Romance* series.

A list of other titles in the *Best Seller Romance* series can be found at the end of this book.

Anne Hampson

A MAN TO BE FEARED

MILLS & BOON LIMITED
15–16 BROOK'S MEWS
LONDON W1A 1DR

First published in Great Britain 1976
by Mills & Boon Limited

This edition 1984

ISBN 0 263 74825 1

Set in Linotype Baskerville 10 on 11½ pt.
02–0884

Made and printed in Great Britain by
Richard Clay (The Chaucer Press) Ltd,
Bungay, Suffolk

CHAPTER ONE

To say that the arrival of Dorian Coralis in the sleepy Dorset village of West Havington had caused a stir would be putting it mildly indeed. It was not only that strangers were rare, but a Greek.... And one so superlatively handsome as this god-like intruder into the indolent tempo of a place where the birth of Mrs Formby's triplets had provided the only excitement in five years....

'He's six-foot-three if he's an inch!' exclaimed Miss Potterton, the postmistress, when, after serving him with a book of stamps, she had watched him stride majestically through the door. 'And as handsome a man as ever entered my shop!'

'Aye,' agreed Mr Godfrey who farmed Green Acres down in the valley, 'I'll wager those two girls up at the Grange are fighting over him.'

'There'll be no fight,' intervened Miss Youdall, who lived with her aged sister in the old mill-house over by the bridge. 'Tanya's got it all her own way with him, just as she has it with others. Who'd want to look at Juliet when there's Tanya around?'

Miss Potterton's nostrils quivered; her pale blue eyes registered disdain.

'Juliet's the nicer of the two, though. She's a sweet child, and I often wonder that she stays with her aunt and uncle at all.'

'She'll be away when she's older,' prophesied Mr Godfrey. 'Little drudge, she is, and always has been since the day the Lowthers decided to take her, when her mam and dad were killed in that accident. Six years old, she was, and I recall that even then they had her with a broom in one hand and a duster in the other.' Which was of course a slight exaggeration on Mr Godfrey's part; nevertheless, it was a known fact throughout the village that Juliet was little more than a servant up at the Grange, the large manor house on the hill overlooking the village green. Her aunt and uncle had surprised everyone by their decision to take the little orphan child into their care; she would be a playmate for their own daughter, they had said, but the fact was that both Tanya and her parents had treated Juliet as an inferior right from the start, and now, at almost seventeen, she had practically the whole of the work of the house on her hands.

'I heard that Tanya and the Greek were seen dining and dancing at the White Swan.' Mrs Goldsmith, who always had a sniff but never a handkerchief, spoke in a kind of conspiratorial manner as, after stuffing into her purse the stamps she had bought, she leant across the counter and said quietly to the postmistress, 'They say that the Lowthers only invited him to stay so that he and Tanya would get together. The Lowthers are comfortably off, as you know, but they're not by any means rich. Now this Dorian Coralis—don't they have odd names in Greece?—this Dorian's the son of a millionaire ship-owner, so it's no wonder they're trying to get Tanya tied up with him.'

'They make a very suited pair, you must admit that.' This came from Mrs Swale, the vicar's housekeeper who, for no apparent reason at all, had never had a good word for Juliet. 'I'd like to see them married myself.'

Mrs Goldsmith gave a loud and unnecessary sniff.

'For my part, I'd sooner see Juliet land him. It'd show Tanya and her parents that Juliet's not such a little outcast after all.'

'Juliet!' exclaimed Mrs Swale with a flash of disdain. 'She's positively ugly——'

'Not ugly!' snapped Mr Godfrey. 'Plain, I'll not deny, but the lass has pretty eyes and a nice peachy skin—sort of,' he ended vaguely.

'She hasn't the poise and confidence of her cousin,' continued Mrs Swale after asking for a postal order. 'Shy and timid—it isn't natural in a girl these days—and I'm not so sure that it's not all put on!'

'Put on!' Mr Godfrey stared belligerently at her and it was clear that he was becoming heated. 'The lass is not yet seventeen! Tanya's twenty-one!'

'And don't forget,' interposed Mrs Goldsmith, 'that Juliet's never been anywhere. Why, they even left her at home last summer when they went off to Greece for their holiday.'

'It was then that they met this fellow, wasn't it?'

'That's right. He and Tanya met somewhere, and Tanya then introduced her parents to him. They must have corresponded and now they've got him over as their guest.'

'You know,' mused Miss Potterton as she stamped the postal order before passing it over the counter to Mrs Swale, 'it struck me right away—when he first arrived over a week ago—that he isn't really their type.'

'What do you mean?' from Mr Godfrey as he lounged against the counter, filling his pipe from a plastic pouch which had seen better days.

'He's so aloof and superior. He's sort of unapproachable, if you know what I'm trying to say?'

'He's a snob, you're meaning?'

'Yes—but also he never smiles no matter how you try to coax him. I should have thought he'd consider the Lowthers far beneath him.'

'Ah, but he's interested in their beautiful daughter, don't forget.'

At this very moment the 'beautiful daughter' was looking at her young cousin with dark furious eyes as she held out a sleek black velvet evening dress, then flung it into Juliet's face.

'I told you last week—when I took it off—that it wanted mending——'

'You didn't, Tanya,' protested Juliet almost in tears. 'You told me to press it with the steam iron, which I did, before hanging it in the wardrobe, but as for——'

'I told you that the hem was coming down! Get it done at once. I'm putting it on tonight!'

'I'm sorry....' Juliet picked up the dress, which had fallen on the floor, and looked at the hem. 'I'll do it right away.'

'And make sure the stitches don't come through on to the right side, because if they do you'll get it done again!' Tanya, dark-haired and possessing an exotic beauty which most men found irresistible, glared at her cousin before, allowing her eyes to rake the slender, immature body, she said scathingly, 'And don't keep making passes at Dorian; it annoys him——'

'I don't make passes! I wouldn't know how!'

'You're plain—Plain Jane we've always called you, and you know why. Dorian considers you to be ugly—do you hear?—ugly! So don't keep on vexing him by trying to make him notice you.'

'I haven't! I——'

'Why did you dye your hair?' demanded Tanya, and she laughed then, a grating sort of laugh that Juliet had always hated.

'I haven't dyed my hair. It's only a rinse.'

The laugh rang out again, echoing all around the elegant bedroom in which Tanya slept.

'When I came back from my holiday I showed you a snapshot of Dorian, remember?'

'Of course.' Juliet's face was pale, her hands icy cold.

'I happened to say that he preferred brunettes to blondes.'

'Well?' Juliet fingered the soft silky velvet of her cousin's dress and for one wild and wonderful moment she herself was wearing it ... and going out to dine and dance with the handsome Dorian Coralis.

'I later told you he was coming to England, on business, but that Mother had invited him to come and stay with us. I mentioned again that he preferred brunettes to blondes, and what did you do, my plain little Emily——?'

'My name's not Emily! I mean, that's one of my names, I know, but I keep asking you all to call me Juliet. People in the village are now obliging enough to call me Juliet.'

'Here, in this house, your name's Emily!—it always has been since the day you arrived——'

'My own mother and father called me Juliet.'

'We don't like it!' Tanya dismissed the matter with a flip of her hand. 'To get back to what we were saying, my *ugly* little *Emily*. What did you do to your hair? Tell me—come on!' Tanya slid forward until her face was close to that of her cousin. The sneering lips were curled, the dark eyes tinged with laughter. 'You poor little fool! You went straight out and bought yourself a hair dye——'

'A rinse!' interrupted Juliet, squirming with shame even before Tanya had finished what she was going to say.

'So what's the difference?' jeered Tanya. 'You'd fallen in love with a photograph—you poor undeveloped little orphan! How he would laugh were I to tell him that, because of what I'd said, you dyed your hair!' Tanya came closer still. 'It didn't do you any good, though, did it? He doesn't even know you're here!'

'Emily!' The loud imperious call came from the direction of the stairs and without a second's delay Judith had the bedroom door open.

'Yes, Aunt Maud?'

'The dog's been sick on the kitchen floor. Go and clean it up! And when you've done that you can fill the coal scuttles ready for tonight!'

'Yes, Aunt Maud.'

Tanya looked at her with an expression of utter contempt.

'You've no guts, have you, Emily?' she said, noting the pallid cheeks, the trembling mouth, the tears that struggled for release. 'You're afraid to answer back——'

'One day, Tanya,' interrupted Juliet in a tight little voice, 'I might just have the courage to *fight* back!' and with that she left the room, her cousin's lovely dress draped over her arm.

She was in the post office the following afternoon, having been sent by Tanya to buy some stamps.

'Hello, Emily—oh, dear, I mean Juliet.' Miss Potterton looked apologetically at her young customer. 'It's a bit difficult, dear, to remember that you want to be called Juliet. We've all been calling you Emily for so long, you see.'

Juliet nodded her head, and although she had already explained it all to Miss Potterton and others in the village, she began to tell her again.

'As you know, I was only six when Aunt Maud and

Uncle Alfred took me in, and as I told you, the names on my birth certificate are Juliet Emily Hardy——'

'Yes, dear, I remember,' interrupted Miss Potterton, but gently. 'There isn't really any need for you to repeat it.'

Juliet swallowed, and hesitated. But then she decided to continue,

'I had always been called Juliet by my parents, but Aunt Maud said she didn't like the name——'

'It's a very pretty name, dear!' interrupted the postmistress rather hotly. 'I can't see how your aunt came to prefer Emily.'

'Well, she did, so she made me take that name and drop Juliet....' Her voice trailed off as with a backswitch of memory she recalled the scene when, having been told she must from now on use the name Emily, Juliet protested tearfully that she didn't like Emily, and in any case, she was used to Juliet.

'You'll do as I say!' snapped her aunt, glaring down at her niece. 'Obedience is the first word you must learn—that and gratitude!' And in order to ensure that the two words were fixed firmly in her mind the woman made her niece sit down and write them out a hundred times, while Tanya, looking into the room now and then, would giggle and sneer, and just as Juliet had finished the piece of work, her cousin took the pen from her hand and scribbled all over the sheet of paper. In consequence Juliet had to do the work again, and just to add insult to injury she was scolded by her aunt for taking so long over the task.

'That was how you all came to know me as Emily.' Juliet spoke at last, but by now there was another customer in the shop—Mr Godfrey.

'Yes,' murmured Miss Potterton. 'I recall that your aunt came in here and said she and her husband had adopted you and that your name was Emily Lowther.'

'It was Juliet Hardy.' Juliet was frowning slightly. 'Some day, Miss Potterton, I shall be known by my own real name, and not by the name that my aunt decided I must use.'

'And you'll be your own colouring too,' put in Mr Godfrey with a frowning glance at Juliet's dark hair. 'Pretty, it was, sort of gold with gingery lights——'

'Auburn lights, Mr Godfrey,' interrupted Juliet gravely. 'It was more fair than dark, as you know, and I wanted it to be like Tanya's.'

'For any particular reason?' he inquired, still frowning.

She fell silent a moment, vividly recalling the way she had felt when Tanya, returning from the holiday in Greece, had shown her the snapshot of Dorian Coralis. Something strange and intangible had stirred within Juliet as she stared down at the hard but handsome features of the man who had been Tanya's constant companion from the moment she had met him a couple of days after her arrival. He had been upset when she left, Tanya had said, and he insisted that they correspond.

'He fell in love with you?' Juliet had asked, still staring at the photograph as if her eyes could not be drawn away.

'Of course! Don't all men fall in love with me, Emily?'

Later, when Juliet learned that Dorian Coralis was to be a guest at the Grange that same strange sensation had come over her and she was filled with a desire to attract his interest, to make herself noticed by him. And so she went out and bought the rinse which, said the chemist who sold it to her, would last until it had gone through several washes. And then he had added,

'Of course, if you don't wash your hair you'll have the colour until it grows out.'

A little cough from Mr Godfrey brought Juliet from her reflections and at the same time reminded her that he was awaiting an answer to his question.

'No—er—not for any particular reason,' she lied. 'I just wanted it to be dark.'

'Well,' said Mr Godfrey, stroking his chin, 'it's my opinion that a lass should be satisfied with what nature gave her.'

A lass should be satisfied with what nature gave her.... Juliet was dwelling on this while Mr Godfrey and Miss Potterton talked. Nature had given her very little, thought Juliet, her eyes focusing mentally on her cousin's impeccably beautiful face. It was the bone structure, she had decided when on beginning to understand such things she had become profoundly aware of the difference in her own looks and those of Tanya. There was nothing she could do about it, so it had been more than a little stupid of her even to entertain the idea that she could attract a man like Dorian Coralis. He had been at the Grange for over a week now and so little conversation had taken place between him and Juliet that she felt he did not even know what her voice was like.

But for Juliet herself, she already knew every line of his face, every muscle that could move either in humour or impatience. She knew the shape of his slender hands, the swing of his lithe body as he walked. His dark eyes were there long after she had lain down in her bed in the attic room over the narrow lower landing; his voice would echo in her ears as slumber claimed her. And in all her dreams he was there.

Mr Godfrey was laughing over something the postmistress had said, Juliet's attention returned to him. His hand was in his pocket; he withdrew some money and placed it on the counter, receiving stamps in return.

'How long is Mr Coralis staying with your aunt and uncle?' It was Miss Potterton who spoke and Juliet said politely,

'I don't know. I believe he has some more business to do in London before he returns to Greece——'

'But he did that before he came here—so I heard.'

Heard.... Juliet had to smile despite the heaviness within her. Miss Potterton heard just about everything that happened for miles around.

'That's right, he did have some business to do before coming to us. But yesterday a letter arrived and after he had read it he said he had some more business to attend to. So he might be going quite soon.'

A small pause and then,

'He works in his father's business, I believe?'

Juliet nodded her dark head.

'Yes, he does. But Tanya says that his father's not at all well and that Dorian practically runs the business.'

'He'll be a very wealthy man one day.'

'I expect he will.'

'You're going to miss him,' from Mr Godfrey. 'He must have been good company for you all?'

Juliet's eyes took on a look of sadness.

'I haven't seen much of him, Mr Godfrey.' Juliet had her purse open and she stepped forward, up to the counter. 'He's Tanya's friend—really.'

Mr Godfrey looked uncomfortable and the postmistress came to his rescue.

'He lives on the island of Rhodes, I believe?'

'He used to, and that's where Tanya met him. He lived in a mansion there.'

'A mansion? I thought they called their houses villas?'

'They do. But Tanya says that Dorian's father's is as large and impressive as a mansion.'

'Doesn't he live with his father now?'

'I think he does sometimes, but I heard him telling Aunt Maud that he wanted to live on an island called Thassos, and he's bought a house there. I think it must be a very beautiful island—from what he says about it.' Juliet's eyes became wistful. 'The villas are all white and have flowers draping the walls and filling the gardens. And the sea is a beautiful blue all the time.'

Mr Godfrey was frowning.

'They should have taken you with them....' His voice trailed off as he realized his lack of tact.

'I can't expect my aunt and uncle to spend money on me for things like that.' The acceptance in her tone only served to make him frown more deeply.

'You haven't ever had a holiday that I can bring to mind,' he said.

'Some day I shall have one, Mr Godfrey.'

'Aye, lass, I reckon you will,' and he glanced sideways at the postmistress who nodded her head in a slow and knowing way. 'Where's the first place you'll choose?'

'Why, Greece, of course,' Juliet replied, and although the sadness in her eyes remained, there was an expression of excitement as well. 'I would like to see the place where Dorian lives.'

Ten minutes later she was walking briskly up the drive leading to the Grange; she had loitered too long in the post office and she was quite prepared for the upbraiding she received from her cousin.

'You're a lazy idle creature!' almost shouted Tanya after already having ranted for a couple of minutes.

'My shoes want cleaning! Get them done—and properly!'

'I always do them properly——'

'And stop answering me back every time I speak! You seem to forget that you're living here on our charity!'

Tanya was in a very bad temper, mused Juliet as she took the shoes down to the kitchen where, in the corner, stood two more pairs of shoes—a pair of her aunt's and a pair of her uncle's. Shoes were always placed in that spot for Juliet to clean, and up till now she had glanced at them with resignation before picking them up and beginning to clean and polish them. But today they bred a resentment so fierce that she could have picked them up and flung them at their owners. If only she could get away! But where would she go? Her 'benefactors' had never given her much money—just barely sufficient for shampoos and toothpaste and the like. Her clothes were all cast-offs tossed to her by Tanya, who was not only taller than Juliet, but a little bigger round the hips. As for the bust—well, Juliet was not yet developed and in consequence the clothes would hang so loosely against her figure that she looked both drab and skinny.

She was busily polishing the shoes when she was interrupted by her aunt's entering the kitchen carrying a tray loaded with soiled table linen.

'Some washing for you,' she said in her harsh manly voice. 'And clean this tray again. You've left polish in the crevices——'

'It's difficult to get out, Aunt Maud. I even used a brush on it——'

'Then use a brush on it again!' snapped her aunt, and left the room. Almost immediately Juliet heard her talking to Tanya in the corridor. 'Don't take it out on us, Tanya. It's your own fault if he hasn't yet asked you to marry him....' The voice faded and Juliet visualized the two—mother and daughter—moving towards the big comfortable sitting-room which looked out on to the lawn.

Something inside Juliet seemed to stab at her heart. Marry.... So Tanya expected Dorian to propose to her. Tanya and Dorian married.... Tanya leaving West Havington to go as a bride to the lovely island of Thassos, an island lying just off the coast of Thrace, an island of flowers and sun and warm sandy beaches backed by coves hollowed out of the rocks by the clear crystal sea.

Tanya as a bride ... Dorian's bride....

'But he hasn't yet asked her to marry him,' whispered Juliet from the depths of a heart that seemed to cry out, of its own accord, 'Don't ask her, Dorian! Don't ask her to marry you—not ever! Wait for me....'

But he never noticed Juliet, and this she had to admit. She was plain, immature, gauche. So very different from Tanya whose beauty had always dazzled any man who happened to come into her company. She was elegant in the way she carried herself, having been taught deportment at the finishing school to which her parents had sent her at the age of seventeen; she spoke and conversed with confidence and knowledge. In short, she suited to perfection the man whose proposal of marriage she hoped to receive. For he too had poise and confidence in plenty; he too spoke in a self-assured manner. He too was superlatively blessed with the gifts which nature could bestow. In appearance, in physique, in nobility of carriage, he surpassed any man whom Juliet had ever seen—or ever would see, she told herself the moment when, after a perfunctory introduction by her cousin, she placed a cold little hand in his and murmured a shy, 'How do you do?' before being told, by the flick of her aunt's finger, to return to the kitchen, from whence she had come in order to be presented as 'our dear little niece whose parents were tragically killed when she was a mite of only six. We took her without hesitation,' her aunt had continued. 'And we've tried to give her the love she lost.'

The clatter of a shoe on the stone floor of the kitchen brought Juliet back to her surroundings, and to her task. But she was soon drifting in thought once again, to that moment when she had first laid her eyes upon Dorian Coralis. The snapshot had already made a deep impression on her, stirring emotions that were both bewildering and exciting, but the actual meeting with the man was little less than devastating. She tried to tell herself that it was impossible to fall in love as swiftly as this; she insisted on describing her emotions as mere pleasure and excitement at the idea of having a visitor from abroad, from a country about which she had read, and where in ancient times gods held sway and pagans worshipped them. It was a mysterious land, and Dorian was a mysterious person, a person with an unusual name and a face that might have been sculptured from stone. But very soon Juliet was forced to accept the truth—that she was irrevocably in love with the dark stranger from Greece; he was her first love, since she had never even been out with a boy—unlike Tanya who had been going out with boys since she was fifteen years of age. But then Tanya had always looked older than her age, and worldly. She had learned the art of make-up at a beauty school in town, and without any learning at all she knew exactly how to use her eyes and her lashes and the other assets given her by prodigal nature.

Juliet had always felt inferior, but not only in looks.

Having had her position drilled into her from as far back as she could remember, she had grown up in the knowledge that she was a pauper, dependent on her aunt and uncle for shelter, for food and clothes, for the security of which she had been robbed by the untimely death of her parents. The constant reminders by her aunt of all that had been done for her, the complaints of her uncle that she failed to display sufficient gratitude and humility, the taunts of her cousin about her plainness, her poverty, and her total lack of confidence ... all these, being perpetual, bordered on persecution, and Juliet would wonder if, and when, escape would eventually come to her. Escape.... It might come at some indeterminate time—or not at all; there was no clear dimension to her future. To compound the drabness and the misery of her life there was the frightening revelation that it could continue until she was a middle-aged spinster, released from bondage only by the deaths of her aunt and uncle.

Yet somewhere in the remoteness of her subconscious a tiny ray of hope survived and in dreams Juliet would see her 'prince' appear, to carry her away from it all, a man who would cherish her, who would protect her, who would shield her from hurt for the rest of her days.

But then she would look in the mirror, and admit that the ray of hope was doomed to die, for who would want a girl as plain and uninteresting as she—Juliet Hardy, whom everyone in the village had called Emily Lowther—until very recently, that was, But when eventually she had had the courage to ask that she be called Juliet, one or two had been kind enough to adhere to her request. But to her aunt she dared not mention her desire, and in consequence Dorian knew her as Emily Lowther and not, as she would have wished, by her real name of Juliet Hardy.

'Emily!' came the voice of Tanya from outside the kitchen door. 'Have you done my shoes yet?' The door was pushed inwards and Tanya stood there, a sneer on her face as she looked down at Juliet, who was kneeling on the floor, rubbing away at one of her uncle's gardening shoes.

'Yes; they're there.' She pointed, but her cousin said arrogantly,

'Then pass them to me!'

Juliet licked her lips, because they had gone dry suddenly. Her throat was also dry, and blocked by a tight little ball of anger. She was becoming bitterly resentful of her treatment, and wildly fluttering about in her brain were the words: 'If only I could marry!'

Dorian Coralis.... Why should his name emerge from the cloud of anger and resentment—and hope?

'It won't hurt you to bend down and pick them up, Tanya,' she said quietly, aware that, should she lose her temper, she would be bound to suffer for it.

'Pass them to me!'

With a shrug Juliet rose to her feet, took a couple of steps and, bending down, picked up the shoes. Tanya snatched them from her hand, and began to examine them. These two actions caused something to snap in Juliet's brain and she said, in a curt, high-spirited voice her cousin had never heard before,

'I'm going to ask Aunt Maud if I can take a secretarial course!'

Tanya stared at her.

'You've asked her before——'

'I'm going to ask her again——' Juliet stopped, her natural caution creeping in on her as she saw her aunt standing in the open doorway.

'What's this I'm hearing, Emily?' demanded the

woman, her dark eyes settling with a hard gaze upon her niece's pallid face.

'I'd l-like to do something, Aunt Maud. The secretarial course I've mentioned once or twice. If I could——'

'We've already been into it. You can't expect your uncle to pay for a secretarial course after all he's done for you already. What an ungrateful child you are, even to suggest he go to so great an expense on your account.'

'I would pay back the money some day——'

'Father's not a millionaire,' broke in Tanya, fingering the buckle on one of the shoes. 'You've cost him enough already.'

Paler than ever, but not yet fully deflated, Juliet explained that it was not unnatural for her to think of the future, and to want to be independent of her uncle.

'I would like to have a place of my own, Aunt Maud,' she added in a pleading voice. 'A little flat which I could furnish as I wanted it to be furnished——'

'So this home's not to your liking?' interposed Tanya in tones of disgust. 'What an ungrateful girl you are, Emily! You seem to forget that you'd have been in an institution if Father and Mother hadn't been so kind as to take you in!'

'I take it,' said Mrs Lowther scathingly, 'that you would like your uncle to pay for a secretarial course for you, so that you could get a post and leave home—taking your salary with you. Emily, I have never in the whole of my life heard of such ingratitude, such utter selfishness.' She turned as her husband joined her. A tall man, he could look over her head, and he now added his stare to those of his wife and daughter. Juliet wanted nothing more than to turn and run from them all. But she said instead, looking at her aunt,

'So I must stay—and remain a servant all my life—an unpaid servant to the three of you?' Still pale, and with her heart beating far too quickly, Juliet voiced this one last protest before being utterly crushed by her uncle, who said sternly,

'Go to your room, Emily! And remain there until you have repented of those words. You may come down only when you are ready to apologize to us all!'

CHAPTER TWO

DORIAN strode along the drive and Juliet's eyes followed as he turned off, to take the path across the lawn towards the summerhouse where she knew Tanya was waiting. Dorian had been out for a walk; Juliet had heard him ask Tanya to accompany him, but she had refused, saying she had things to do. Immediately he had left the house she went up to her bedroom, where she was to spend the next three quarters of an hour making herself up, brushing her hair, and putting on the dress which, in Juliet's opinion, was far too daring in every way. As low as could be, the bodice did not even have shoe-string straps to keep it in place. It was boned, and very tight, and it revealed her bronzed back and shoulders, and the lovely curve of her throat. It was short, with slits up the sides, and although she had to admit that her cousin looked gloriously attractive in it Juliet decided that this was one dress which failed to incite her envy. She had seen Tanya saunter over to the summerhouse and knew that Dorian would eventually meet her there.

It was over an hour later that the couple emerged and Juliet watched them from the dining-room window. Dorian was cool, his head arrogantly held, as usual; Tanya on the other hand was slightly dishevelled, and her face was flushed. As she drew close to the window Juliet caught her expression, and saw the dreamy shadows in her lovely eyes.

This was love, she thought, even now too naïve to grasp the real relationship existing between the two. All she knew was that she was fiercely, burningly jealous of her cousin, that she herself wanted Dorian's kisses and his embrace, his strong lithe body close to hers.

Why should she give up? True, she was plain, but she knew of girls in the village who were just as plain, and they had managed to find the kind of happiness which she, Juliet, now desired.

Tanya went off and for some reason Dorian came into the sitting-room and spoke a few words to Juliet, mentioning the pretty walk along by the village pond. Overwhelmed by this small degree of attention he was affording her, Juliet could only give him a shy fluttering smile and after a rather awkward silence he once again spoke conversationally to her.

'What have you been doing today, Emily?' His voice was low, and faintly accented, a voice Juliet had come to love. 'I haven't seen you around.'

He never saw her, she could have pointed out, but of course she did not do so. Instead, she smiled again, and fluttered her eyelashes and tried to be coy and experienced all in one pitiful attempt to hold his interest.

'I've been busy in the garden,' she told him, and then wished she hadn't because his very dark eyes fell to her hands—hands rough and cracked by hard work. He seemed to frown, she thought, as if he hated to see a girl with so disgustingly ill-cared-for hands. She closed them, swallowing hard. 'Wh-what have you been d-doing?'

'Writing letters, and walking in the village.'

'You like our village?'

'Very much.' Dorian stifled a yawn and glanced towards the door.

'Tanya won't be long,' she just had to say, for the sole purpose of noting his reaction. His eyes remained devoid of expression as he said,

'If I know Tanya she'll be half an hour repairing her

make-up.' He sat down, and Juliet also found a seat.

What a thing to say! Juliet detected a note of contempt in his voice and wondered greatly at it.

'You and Tanya get along very well together.' She spoke awkwardly, scarcely knowing what to say to him. He was so superior, so overpowering, sitting there on the couch, one leg crossed over the other. The classically-etched contours of his face were set in cold forbidding lines, his lean jaw was taut, his mouth—that sensuous mouth which she desired to feel against her own—was set, unsmiling.

No question of it—he was like some all-powerful god, invincible, unapproachable.

Unapproachable....

Tanya could get close to him ... so why not I? thought Juliet.

'Naturally we get along well together.' The answer came tardily, and accompanied by a gleam of amusement in his eyes. The lips curved and Juliet frowned because she disliked the way they curved; she gained the impression that Dorian was a cynical kind of man, and this hurt in a way she failed to understand.

'Dorian,' she said suddenly, 'will you walk with me in the garden?'

He stared, surprised.

'If you like,' he said, and Juliet's heart leapt almost into her throat. Warmth spread all over her body and a tender smile curved her lips.

'Thank you.' She rose and, looking up at him, she saw the sheer amusement written on his handsome features.

'Which way, Emily?' The tone was soft, and it scared her a little. 'Do you definitely want to keep to the garden?'

'The woods are nice to walk in when it's been fine

and sunny like this.' What was she doing? She wished with all her heart that she had some experience of men.

'The woods, eh?' Was his voice grim now—or did she imagine it? 'Which way do you enter them?'

'You haven't been in the woods with Tanya?' She was excited, awaiting his reply. And when she received it she said impulsively, 'Oh, I'm glad, then, because it means that you and I have something of our own—something secret, doesn't it?'

Dorian frowned as he looked down at her.

'You're a strange girl, Emily,' he said, and his stride seemed to become longer so that she was almost running to keep pace with him.

'In what way strange, Dorian?' She assumed an artlessness which seemed to anger him.

'I shouldn't have imagined your wanting to walk in the woods with a man. In my country you'd have felt your father's whip about your backside.'

She stopped dead, looking up at him with a face fusing with colour—vivid crimson colour.

'Oh,' she quivered, 'I didn't like your saying a thing like that to me!'

'I didn't expect you would. Come on, if we're to have our walk!'

'Are you angry with me?' she queried after a while.

'Just what are you trying to do?' he wanted to know, sending her a sideways glance.

She could not answer, simply because there was no answer. She had no idea what she was trying to do.

'There's a path,' she said, changing the subject, and pointing as she did so. 'It leads to a brook and a small waterfall.'

Dorian was silent, but he seemed to be deep in thought, because there was a strange furrow on his low and noble forehead.

They took the path . . . and she touched his hand. He glanced down and she snatched hers away, but a few seconds later she ventured to slip her hand into his.

'You don't mind?' she asked, and her voice was a trifle husky because she was so unsure of herself . . . and because her heart was racing. She was scared, ecstatically scared. Her face was lifted and she pleaded with her eyes. She wanted him to stop, to put his arms around her, and to kiss her . . . passionately, savagely.

She wanted him to desire her.

'And supposing I do mind?' Anger mingled with amusement in the look he gave her.

'I've never held a man's hand,' she said, still trotting to keep up with him. 'It's . . . pleasant.'

'Never?' he repeated sceptically. 'You expect me to believe that—after you've invited me into the woods?'

'It's true.' She should by rights be taking offence, evincing indignation, but she was too afraid of angering him to the point where he would want to return to the house. In which event they would walk along without speaking, and the strain would increase until she would be so miserable she would want to die.

'Tell me,' he was saying about five minutes later when, having come to a stop by a huge oak tree, he had pushed her towards it and now stood facing her, 'what do you want me to do?'

'Kiss m-me. . . .' She dropped her head and waited. There was a long and painful silence before, tilting her face up with a finger under her chin, Dorian bent his head and kissed her on the lips. She quivered like a frightened bird; he felt her body shake and, bringing her towards him, he put his arms around her and the next moment she was experiencing the passionate pressure of his body, was responding immaturely to his kiss, a kiss which left her mouth rosy, and bruised.

Her childhood had gone—for ever.

He released her and held her from him.

'Did you like that?' Grim tones and curt. 'Well?'

'Yes, Dorian, I did.' She clung to him, trying to convey the fact that she loved him. In her immaturity it did not occur to her that he, being a man of the world, did not believe in love. She was not to know that in his country love rarely entered into marriage. She was too inexperienced to guess that he was filled with contempt for her, that where she was offering love he believed she was offering her body, offering it with the abandonment with which the other girl of the household offered hers.

She was not to know that her love would turn to hatred—to bitter hatred that would consume her to the point where all she desired was to bring him to the dust.

He kissed her again and then, abruptly,

'Come, let's get back!'

'But we've not been out many minutes,' she protested.

'Let's go back, I said.' Quiet the tones now but firm. Juliet fell meekly into step beside him, her mind bewildered by his curtness after so intimate and beautiful a scene of lovemaking. She supposed it had been lovemaking—that warm embrace and the passionate, demanding kisses. In all her drab life this had been the shining moment; she would remember it for ever.

'Dorian,' she faltered when they were approaching the house, 'you're not angry about anything, are you?'

'Shut up!' he snapped.

'But——'

'No, I'm not angry!'

'You sound angry.' She rubbed a hand across her

eyes; he would not have much patience for her tears, she thought, yet a tiny sob escaped her as she added, 'It was so wonderful, Dorian. Didn't you think so too?'

He glanced down into her childish, immature face, and he was frowning strangely. He seemed puzzled by her, as if he could not decide what to make of her behaviour.

He was not to know that she had been lonely all her life, an outcast in the home into which she had been forced to live, a servant, and the first and foremost emotion expected of her was gratitude. He was not to know how his attention, for those few moments, had been to her like a draught of heady wine. He was not to know that her young heart was starved, so starved that, until now, she had scarcely known what the word love meant, simply because she had never experienced love, nor received it.

If he had realized all these things he might have acted differently from what he did ... and Juliet might never have come to hate him.

It was Sunday morning and the church bells rang out; the hills were covered with snow, shining white and pure in the January sunshine. Juliet could smell bacon cooking, and the delicious odour of coffee being percolated.

She came into the breakfast-room clad in a pretty dressing-gown which fastened snugly to her lovely throat.

'Happy birthday!'

'Thank you, Meg; oh, but the food smells good!'

'Doesn't my cooking always smell good?' Meg, tall and well-made, grinned cheerfully and nodded towards a box which was wrapped in pretty red and gold paper. 'For you. The card's inside as well. No sense in posting it when your birthday's on a Sunday.' She paused, then added, 'Have a happy year, Juliet.'

'Thank you,' Juliet said again, and picked up the parcel. 'Meg—you shouldn't have——!' she was saying a moment later.

'I wanted to! It's silver, not plated.'

'I can see that.'

'How very beautiful!' Juliet picked up the silver-backed brush and took it through her hair, hair that shone in its natural colour of deep gold, with copper tints which were highlighted by the low slanting rays of the winter sun. 'I've never owned anything quite like this.' She picked up the mirror and looked into it. She smiled happily at what she saw.

'I decided on it over three months ago, when I had that win on the pools.'

'It was only a small win, Meg.'

'Juliet, love, I wanted to buy it—have wanted to show gratitude for a long while, because you let me share your house.'

'Gratitude.' Frowningly Juliet shook her head. 'Never mention the word, Meg dear, please!'

Meg looked strangely at her, but when she spoke it was merely to say that she would bring in the breakfast.

'I'm glad you did as you were told and stayed in bed until it was ready,' she was saying a moment later as she entered with the tray. 'Today's all yours; I'm at your service for the whole of it!' They both laughed at this and presently they were sitting opposite to one another at a table by the window, from where they could see the small but well-kept garden with its lawn and flower borders and those shrubs which give pleasure in the winter time, either by their foliage or by the bright red and orange-coloured berries they bore.

'Twenty-five,' murmured Juliet with a faint smile.

'What a long way I've come since then!'

Meg looked curiously at her but made no comment. She poured the coffee, exclaiming when it dripped on to the cloth which she had put on clean that morning, especially for the occasion of her friend's birthday.

'Drat! My pet hate is a coffee pot that drips! I should have used yours!'

'Mine's just the same.'

Meg passed her her cup of coffee, a frown touching her brow as she glanced again at the brown mark on the cloth.

'Yes,' she said, 'my pet hate.' But her ill-humour vanished and she laughed. 'What's your pet hate, Juliet?'

A small moment of total silence ensued before Juliet said, in a tone her friend had never heard before,

'A man called Dorian Coralis.'

'A man? But you never bother with men!'

'I've been out with one or two,' corrected Juliet. 'It was before you came here to share the house with me.'

'This man—is he English?'

'He's a Greek.'

'You've been to Greece? Is that where you met him?'

'I met him in England. He was here on a visit.' Juliet became reflective, mechanically cutting the bacon which lay on the plate before her. She forgot Meg's presence as she repeated to herself, 'Yes, I've come a long way since then.' And her eyes were hard suddenly with an expression her friend had noticed several times before—if Juliet happened to be in a pensive mood. After a small hesitation Meg ventured to say,

'I've been with you for over two years, Juliet, and you've never told me much about your life?' She ended on an apologetic note, but Juliet smiled reassuringly at her and said,

'What do you want to know, Meg?'

'Oh—er—nothing much——'

'I feel like talking, but it's a long story and you might find it boring.'

'I don't believe I will.' Meg helped herself to more bacon from the heavy silver-plated dish which she had placed on a dinner-wagon by her side. 'Don't talk unless you really want to,' she added, but the note of curiosity in her voice could not be concealed.

Juliet's eyes again became reflective. She began to talk, stopping now and then to sip her coffee or pop a piece of toast into her mouth. At length she made a longer pause.

'You were having it pretty grim by this time,' said Meg, and Juliet nodded her head.

'Grim is a mild word for my life with those people,' she said but, strangely, not one hint of bitterness entered her voice. But it did later, as she began to bring Dorian Coralis into the picture, telling Meg about the snapshot which had had such a startling effect on her.

'Although Tanya had declared that he was in love with her I desperately wanted him to notice me, and as she had said that he preferred brunettes I coloured my hair——'

'Coloured that beautiful hair!' Meg broke in to exclaim. 'You must have been out of your tiny mind!'

'I was certainly that,' came the grim response. 'I was very soon head over heels in love with the man.' She could look without embarrassment into Meg's face. Yes, Juliet had come a long way since that first painful experience of love. 'I never did stand a chance, of course,' she added musingly. 'Tanya was dazzlingly beautiful while I was plain—ugly in fact.' She almost laughed at Meg's expression as she said this, and she awaited her verbal response with some considerable amusement.

'But you could never have been plain—*never!*'

The silver-backed mirror was on the sideboard, close enough for Juliet to reach out and pick it up. She held it before her and smiled. She was far from being vain, but she knew that she was very beautiful. The mirror was returned to the sideboard and another small silence fell before Juliet continued, her narrative now a little more difficult; but her voice remained perfectly steady for all that, as she related the incident in the woods.

'He must have thought you were throwing yourself at him,' asserted Meg when eventually her friend paused.

'I admit it, but still find no excuse for what he did as a result of my little hour of foolishness.'

'Before you go on,' interposed Meg interestedly, 'tell me: did he marry your cousin?'

'Greek men never marry their mistresses,' she replied. 'However, at the time, I was led by Tanya to believe that he had asked her to marry him. I was shattered, Meg, and wept enough tears to swell that stream out there. Every night I cried myself to sleep. It was a devastating time, and I wouldn't wish a similar one on my worst enemy.'

'Did you know at that time that they were lovers?'

Juliet shook her head.

'Had I been older I'd have seen it at once. Being young—a very young seventeen, Meg, because I'd never been out of the village since I was six, and I'd never even gone out with a boy—I saw no real wickedness in their association. I suppose I imagined they just kissed and cuddled, over there in that summerhouse.' Her voice held not only bitterness but contempt as well. 'Whatever his opinion of me, he'd have discovered, eventually, that I was very different from my cousin.

She had given herself to him within hours of meeting him.'

Meg glanced at her in surprise.

'How did you learn that?' she wanted to know.

'I was in the garden one evening and it was dark. I heard her say "What bliss we had, Dorian—and after only a few hours' acquaintanceship." But of course I didn't catch on to her meaning until I'd grown up a bit and seen a little of the world.'

'You were about to tell me what he had done as a result of your little hour of foolishness, as you termed it?'

'Yes. . . .' Juliet fell silent after uttering that one slow word, and she reached for the butter, helping herself to a pat which she put on to her side-plate. 'He didn't act at first, of course, for otherwise I'd never have been there to hear her talking to him in the garden, nor would I have heard from her lips the lie about his asking her to marry him. However, he mistook my glances—which I couldn't help giving him——'

'Loving glances?'

'Yes, they were the sort that misled him into believing that he could have me, body and soul, just whenever he wished.'

'And you, in your innocence, were all unsuspecting of this?'

'Of course. And as I was about to say, he took these glances the wrong way and decided to approach my aunt and uncle, to warn them that if they didn't take me in hand then I'd bring them trouble in plenty, and before very long. He said he himself could have had me—that I threw myself at him after brazenly asking him to take me into the woods—but respect for them as his hosts had forbidden me to take advantage of my offer. However, he assured them that, unless they did something, there would be others, and in plenty——'

'Oh, Juliet! How perfectly hateful of him! Why, you're the most decent girl I've ever met!'

Juliet shrugged at this and, looking down, picked up her knife and buttered her toast.

'From what I've told you of my aunt and uncle you can imagine what the result was. Dorian said I needed a whipping——' Here Juliet stopped and coloured painfully. 'This is what would have happened to me in his country. I truly believe my uncle would have taken his advice had I not been given the strength to threaten him with retaliation. I told him I'd go straight to the police station.'

'What happened then?'

'I was crucified by their scorn and contempt. They kept on at me for days and days. Dorian had gone by now, but the daily tirade continued. To make matters worse Tanya spread the tale all over the village so that people who had once stopped to smile and chat merely gave me a hurried greeting and passed on. The climax came one day when, as I'd gone to the shop for my aunt, a hateful greasy-haired youth waylaid me in a lonely place and tried—tried——' Juliet could not continue and Meg said swiftly:

'Skip it; I'm not without imagination. You escaped, obviously.'

'I had to cry out in the end. He put his hand over my mouth and told me to stop acting, as everyone in the village knew what I was.' Again she stopped, and to her amazement she saw tears in her friend's dark eyes. 'The cry had been heard by a Mr Godfrey; a friend he had always been,' she digressed and her voice almost broke. 'He came to my rescue, but I always wondered if he considered that I'd got only what I deserved.' She fell silent and for a space both girls attended to the food before them. 'Life became unbearable,' Juliet continued at length. 'But I had scarcely any money at all. You see, the stoppage of my pocket money was the first thing they did by way of punishment.'

'I don't suppose they ever gave you much, anyway?'

'Barely enough to buy the necessities like toothpaste and toilet soap and shampoos. However, I did manage to save out of the pittance and so, with about ten pounds in my purse, I packed my bag and, one night after they had all gone to bed, I crept from the house and came out into the world.'

'With nowhere to go?'

Juliet shook her head and for a moment distress shadowed her lovely eyes. The memory of that night was not one she wished to revive.

'And no friends or relatives. In my heart, Meg, was a bitter hatred for that man because it was all his doing.'

'What hateful, hateful people they all were! I only wish they could see you now, and discover what a success you've made of your life.' Meg glanced around the pretty room, but seeing this action Juliet lifted a hand.

'This house was left to me, remember. I did mention that to you. I haven't earned it, Meg.'

'When you said it was left I thought it was by a relative?' Meg's eyes were questioning and Juliet said, rising from her chair,

'I'll make some more coffee. I warned you it would be a long story.' She smiled as she took up the coffee pot. 'You haven't heard one half of it yet, Meg.'

When she returned with the freshly-made coffee Juliet poured it into the cups and then, sitting down in her chair, she resumed her story.

'It was very late when I left my uncle's house and as

black as pitch, for there was neither moon nor stars——'

'But weren't you terrified? I know I would have been!'

'I was so scared that my teeth rattled, but I knew I must make my escape from those terrible people—not only my own relatives at the Grange but everyone in the village, for I was branded, Meg. You have no idea how evil a thing gossip is when it's spread around a tiny place like that. It gathers untruths with every telling until, in the end, the original story would hardly be recognised at all.'

Meg nodded understandingly, but all she said was,

'Go on, Juliet. I've never heard anything quite so interesting—and heartrending—as this.'

'Don't pity me,' rejoined Juliet. 'It was the best thing that happened to me, although you might not think so in a moment.' She paused to take a sip of her steaming coffee. 'I made for the railway station, which was about a mile and a quarter from the Grange. The last train to Manchester was due at a quarter to one and I managed to catch it.'

'Didn't anyone see you—and ask questions?'

'One or two dogs barked as I walked along in the dark and in consequence their owners drew back the curtains or opened their doors. But they couldn't see me and no one spoke. I reached the station just as the train was coming in. The porter knew me, of course, and was eyeing my suitcase suspiciously. I placed the correct money down and asked for a ticket, and as the train was in the station he had no time to ask questions. I was aboard it before he knew what was happening, but I suspected he would instantly telephone my uncle, just to make sure nothing was amiss. So I got off the train one stop before Manchester and caught the electric, which put me down at another station altogether. So if the railway officials *had* been alerted, and tried to find me as I got off that train, they were wasting their time.'

'You foiled them all!' intervened Meg excitedly. 'And you only a mere babe, as it were! Go on. What happened next?'

'I was lucky enough to get another train, this time to Rugby.'

'But why Rugby?'

'Money, Meg. The fares took most of my money. I was left with less than two pounds in my purse.'

'Lord—how awful!' Meg was actually sitting up straight, biting her fingernails and, diverted, Juliet gave a gay little laugh and said that it was all water under the bridge now. 'I know,' nodded Meg, 'but it makes me shudder.'

'There were quite a lot of people at Rugby, despite the hour, so no one took too much notice of a young girl. I went into the waiting-room and lay down—others were doing the same, so I was not in any way conspicuous. The following morning I went forth, intending, I suppose, to book in at a cheap guest-house for the night, leave my bag, and then go out and try to find a job.'

'You poor little thing! Oh, Juliet, I'm very much afraid I'm going to cry!'

'Nonsense! What is there to cry about?'

'Nothing now,' owned Meg sheepishly, but she seemed impelled to add, her voice choking a little already, 'But there was at that time. Whatever did you do?'

'I landed myself in hospital.'

'You——?' Meg blinked at her. 'How did you manage that?'

'It's all so vague, Meg. I suppose I was distraught

despite the fact that I had some sort of a plan in mind. But I recall feeling terribly lost and alone. It was like being in a net of isolation and you want to fling out your arms to escape, or to cry out—to scream, even. No one who hasn't been through such an experience can even begin to imagine what it's like. I was wandering, floundering, desperately trying to keep calm.'

'And in your heart was a terrible fear,' stated Meg, and after she had spoken a strange silence fell upon the room.

'Also a terrible hatred, Meg. A black and all-enveloping hatred—of Dorian Coralis. He had caused it all—oh, I know that I'd have left them some time. I knew it even before the persecution began. But I intended to make plans, not to run away into a void of uncertainty like that. Yes, Meg, stronger than any other emotion at that time was this venomous hatred of that man.' Juliet took up her cup and drank some of the delicious contents. 'I don't remember stepping into the road in front of a bus——'

'A bus! Oh, my God!'

'They told me at the hospital that they thought I was wanting to commit suicide. Witnesses said the same. It would seem that I literally walked off the pavement, right across the path of the oncoming bus.'

'And?' breathed Meg, her coffee going cold by her elbow, which was now resting on the table, while her finger ends were still between her lips.

'Among other injuries there was a most terrible facial disfigurement.' She stopped there to allow this to sink in; Meg was already nodding her head from side to side, her eyes wandered significantly to the mirror on the sideboard.

'I'm beginning to see,' she said. 'Plastic surgery?'

'Yes. I really was plain before the accident—ugly,

almost, as I've already explained. Well, I had one operation after another on my face and neck, apart from the repairing of injuries on other parts of my body. The surgeon seemed to be accepting a challenge, and I knew that he actually enjoyed working on me.' She paused reflectively and a smile hovered on her lips. 'He was like an artist determined to produce a work of perfection.'

'And he certainly did!'

Softly Juliet flushed.

'I know he did,' she returned simply, and her admission was in total tribute to the man she had to thank for her appearance as it was today. 'The whole thing took over ten months,' continued Juliet, going on to explain that although she was at times questioned as to where she had come from, she had managed to avoid mentioning her guardians. 'Fortunately for me my handbag had been stolen in the hubbub of the accident, so I had no papers at all. My suitcase contained nothing but my clothes. I pretended I had lost my memory, and as I was so ill I was not troubled too much at all.'

'But surely the doctors began doing something about your memory?'

'The surgeon doing the operation was greatly feared by everyone—he would think nothing of raving at a member of the staff if something didn't suit him. And he gave strict orders that I was not to be questioned, or troubled mentally in any way whatsoever. My life was to be made easy so that I would relax all the time and therefore my features would remain tranquil. So, for the most part, I was left alone. However, he did allow the welfare people to come to me—later, of course, when I was almost ready to leave the hospital. They found me a marvellous job with an elderly couple. I lived in their home; they grew to love me, treating me like a daughter. They had no relatives at all. . . .' She tailed off, glancing round the cosy, well-furnished room, and the light of perception flashed into her friend's eyes.

'They left you this house. It was they who gave you back your self-respect. Perhaps they paid for an education?' Juliet nodded and, delighted with her deductions, Meg took up her coffee cup and drank the entire contents.

'The idea at first, Meg, was that I be a sort of housekeeper for them—Mrs Manley had recently had a stroke and couldn't do anything at all—doing the shopping and cooking, and helping the daily woman with the washing and the chores. But very soon they were wanting to know all about me, and as I liked them so much I confided everything. It was after this that they told me they would like to regard me as a daughter and not as a servant. They offered me an education at a private school for young ladies and it was there that I took the secretarial course I'd always dreamed of. They got another daily woman in, but I was always there at night and at the week-ends. I never went out, because I considered it my duty to be there, at hand, if either of them should need me. In any case,' she added with a sweet and tender smile, 'I was so happy to be with them that I never had any desire to go out in the evenings even though they often urged me to do so.'

'You made a complete break with the old life,' murmured Meg. 'You must have felt pretty good about that,'

'I did,' was Juliet's heartfelt response. 'I was using my own name; I had a new identity. I knew that my aunt and uncle were unable to contact me in any way.'

'A complete break....' Meg repeated what she had said, her brow furrowed in thought. 'New name, new face, new life.' She looked at Juliet and shook her head, marvelling at the beauty of her features. 'If as you say, you were plain, then they'd never recognise you even if they did happen to meet up with you?'

'No. I didn't recognize myself. Of course, the surgery was done gradually, by a series of operations, and so I didn't receive any sort of a shock. However, when I compared myself with a snapshot I had—well, I'll go and get it and you'll then understand what I mean.' She went out and Meg heard her running up the stairs. She was a little flushed and breathless when she returned. 'There it is. You must admit that I was a plain Jane, to say the least.'

Meg gazed and gazed, repeatedly lifting her eyes to Juliet's face.

'It's ... incredible,' she breathed. 'What an amazing transformation! Gosh, one could almost declare that it was worth it—the process by which the transformation came about, I mean.'

'At the time I didn't think so, naturally. But as progress was made and I saw what was happening, I began to feel excited——'

'And who wouldn't!'

'No, not about the transformation specifically. I saw that here was a way to become totally free. Not that they could ever have forced me to return to the Grange, but I seemed to derive a strange satisfaction from the knowledge that, if I wished, I could confront any or all of them and they wouldn't know that I was the girl they had persecuted.'

'Yes,' nodded Meg thoughtfully. 'I know exactly what you mean.' She placed the snapshot down at last, but still kept her eyes upon it. 'Your hair was dark when this was taken,' she observed, and Juliet nodded her head.

'Dorian took it—I don't know why. When it was developed he gave it to me.'

'So this Dorian knew you as a plain girl with dark hair?'

'He also knew me as Emily Lowther, the name my aunt and uncle forced me to use.' Leaning forward in her chair, Juliet took up the coffee pot and poured herself another drink. It would be cold, she thought abstractedly, but she put sugar and milk in it just the same. When at length she lifted her head Meg saw the hardness that glinted in her eyes.

Dorian Coralis.... Juliet's heart was as hard as stone at this moment; her benefactors, Mr and Mrs Manley, would never have believed her capable of such hardness, or of such black hatred as she had for the man who had not only brought her to the depths of humiliation but who had also been responsible for the pain and misery she had later endured. What, she wondered, would he think of Juliet Hardy, the fair-haired beauty who, because she had known the love of that aged couple, had blossomed in an altogether different way, becoming self-assured, confident, gay? She had received an education, and since the deaths of her benefactors within three months of one another four years after she had come to them, she had had a pleasant social life, mixing with other girls like herself, and their boy-friends. She was eagerly received in their homes and invited to anything that happened in the way of parties and other functions.

She was, however, still inexperienced where the fundamentals of love were concerned, but she was no longer the shy and gauche creature who, because of Dorian's malicious denouncement, had suffered so dreadfully, even losing the high opinion of the people of the village, a position she had enjoyed and which had made life a little more bearable. For, as she had told Meg, she could always be sure of a chat in the post office or along the lane with someone from the village. Often she would hear someone say,

'Come on in, lassie. I've just made a cup of tea.'

All this had ceased ... owing to the action of Dorian Coralis. Again that hardness entered her eyes and, watching her, Meg gave a small sigh and her forehead furrowed in a frown. She thought: 'What a shame she has this hatred. Only softness and tenderness should look out from the eyes of a girl with so sweet a disposition as that of Juliet.'

CHAPTER THREE

'I CAN'T understand why those people—your aunt and uncle—took you in the first place.' Meg and Juliet were still at the table, more coffee having been made, this time by Meg. 'They obviously didn't act either from a sense of duty or of love.'

'My aunt couldn't have any more children; she told someone that as Tanya was going to be lonely she decided to take me when my parents were killed.' Juliet thought of the many occasions when she had been blamed for what Tanya had done, and she recalled the difference made when it came to things like Christmas presents, outings, or clothes. Tanya's presents had always been more expensive than those given to Juliet. And for the most part Juliet had worn her cousin's cast-off clothes, but on the rare occasion she had had something new. Her aunt would then repeatedly remind Juliet of the expense, and that she ought to be eternally grateful that she had been provided for in this way.

'We had no need to take you,' her aunt would say. 'It was done out of kindness. You're a big expense to your uncle, and you must never forget it.'

That, Juliet would say, but to herself, was impossible. She was never given an opportunity to forget, being so constantly reminded of her position. Her cousin had been sent to the school in town, going on the train each day, whereas Juliet had gone to the village school. Tanya had been given the opportunity of training for a career, something that was denied to Juliet.

'You'll not require to be trained,' her aunt would say,

'because you're to stay at home and work in the house.'

A servant for a few pence a week, reflected Juliet bitterly. Yet at the same time a feeling of deep satisfaction swept over her, for she had made her escape—and now her aunt and uncle would have to pay a maid a proper wage . . . or else do without one. Suddenly she was filled with the urge to go back to West Havington, just for a few hours, to talk to people and discover what had happened since she had left nearly eight years ago. She would cause a stir because she would be a stranger there, just as Dorian Coralis had been a stranger. Many changes must have taken place, she mused, thinking again of Dorian Coralis . . . and of his affair with her cousin. Were they married? It was possible but highly improbable, for, as she had told Meg, Greek men were known never to marry their mistresses.

'How old will this Dorian be now?' inquired Meg as the thought occurred to her.

'Thirty-four; he was twenty-six at the time.'

'Oh—quite young, then? I had imagined him to be much older than that.'

'He was old enough in the mind,' was Juliet's retort, spoken in accents of contempt. 'Dorian Coralis was a man of the world then, so what he's like now I wouldn't like to guess.'

'Probably gone all cynical where women are concerned—or else he's settled down and is married to a cosy little wife who's given him several children.'

An almost harsh laugh issued from Juliet's lips, a laugh that grated on her friend's ears so that she frowned and wished she had not uttered words that were to produce that laugh.

'He'd probably find a life like that exceedingly dull and boring, and he'd soon go off and find himself a pillow friend——'

'A what?'

'That's the delicate name they're given over there in Greece. Yes, he'd soon be unfaithful to his wife, of that I'm sure.'

Meg looked curiously at her.

'And yet you fell in love with him,' she said.

'At that time he was a sort of god in my estimation. I fell for his looks and his physique and didn't question what lay underneath. I was too young, too naïve.' Again the laugh was heard. 'I hadn't even been kissed, Meg!'

'You'll always hate him, won't you, Juliet?'

'Always!' The hand resting on the table closed, slowly and tightly. The light in her eyes became a fierce ember, fanned by her emotion, and Meg was profoundly conscious of the fact that it could burst into flame just whenever Juliet wanted it to. 'If I ever have the opportunity of paying him back,' added Juliet, 'I shall not hesitate to do so. In fact, I'd go to extreme lengths to make him suffer, to bring him lower than the dust in the gutter!'

'Juliet—girl! This isn't you!'

'Don't be alarmed,' said Juliet, and like a miracle her whole expression changed and she gave a tinkling little laugh, the kind of laugh with which Meg had, over the last two years, become familiar. 'I'm no Jekyll-and-Hyde.'

'All the same,' said Meg on a little troubled note, 'I sincerely hope that you and he never come face to face again.'

'I don't expect we shall. He lives in Greece and I'm not likely to go there. Even if I did it would be a million to one chance of our ever meeting each other.' Her voice was quiet and calm. She was indifferent to Dorian

Coralis, as she was most of the time. For he had become a figure whose image it was difficult to bring into focus, and with every passing year he became more and more remote until, lately, he had become a nebulous shadow of a past she had no desire to recall. But on rare occasions he would become startlingly real; she would see those finely-etched contours of his face as clearly as if he had only a moment ago left her presence. She would see him bend to kiss her ... she would actually find herself putting a finger to her lips, because they seemed to hurt a little from the contact of his own demanding mouth.

'Although I don't ever want you to meet him,' Meg was saying, 'there's no doubt that it would be a most diverting experience for you.' Amusement edged her tone and Juliet smiled in response, her lovely eyes registering a twinkle of humour.

'Indeed it would,' she agreed readily.

'There's your voice, of course, but that in itself wouldn't give you away.'

'I expect that in eight years even that's changed. In any case, he wouldn't remember what it was like, since he scarcely ever spoke to me. It was not the plain, nondescript little housemaid he was interested in, but the glamorous daughter of the house.'

'This aunt and uncle,' mused her friend curiously, 'were they wealthy too?'

'They weren't in the same class as Dorian, but they were the richest people in West Havington. My uncle was regarded as the squire and people used to treat him with great respect.' Juliet paused a moment. 'Meg,' she said at length, 'how would you like to come with me to West Havington some time? I've an urge to go back and take a look at the village.'

'I'd love to go with you!' accepted Meg without a second's hesitation.

Many changes had occurred in the village; building had taken place on a fairly large scale and one of the first things Juliet saw was that the row of cottages where both Mrs Goldsmith and Miss Youdall had lived had been pulled down in order to facilitate the widening of the road.

'So much for the "sleepy little village" you described to me,' said Meg as, sitting beside Juliet in the car, she glanced away to her left, to the large estate of modern bungalows which followed the contours of the undulating land.

'That was Mr Godfrey's farm,' returned Juliet with a deep regretful sigh. 'I wonder where he is now?'

'Probably retired and living like a lord on all the money he got for his land.'

Juliet pulled up outside the post office.

'It's a bit different,' she said, examining it with a critical eye. 'Someone's added a room on that end, and there's a garage now. I can't think that Miss Potterton would do that, so it must have changed hands. Let's go and see.'

They got out of the car and entered the post office. As Juliet had thought, it was a stranger who stood behind the counter. Juliet bought some stamps and then asked,

'Has Miss Potterton retired?'

The man looked oddly at her.

'She's been dead these past five years.'

'Oh ... I'm sorry.' Turning without another word, Juliet left the shop, Meg following closely behind her. 'She was kind to me,' explained Juliet simply as she brushed a tear from her eye.

'Perhaps,' said Meg seriously, 'you shouldn't have come.'

'I want to see the Grange. Do you mind walking? It isn't far – just beyond the woods, over there.' She pointed, her memory clear and vivid. The woods.... Where Dorian had kissed her and held her in his arms....

They had been walking a mere few minutes when Juliet stopped, amazement and a kind of horror mingling in her voice as she exclaimed,

'Those houses—they're on my uncle's land!'

'You mean he'll have sold some of his land for building?'

'He always swore he'd never have any building near his home....' Juliet's voice trailed away as she saw what had really happened. 'The houses are on the land adjoining his.'

'And by golly,' exclaimed Meg as she and Juliet turned into a bend in the road, 'they've ruined his view absolutely!'

'He'd have been furious—out of his mind, almost. He adored that view over to the lake from the hills.' A few low bushes prevented Juliet from seeing more at the moment, but presently she was standing still, gasping in disbelief. 'The Grange is almost surrounded by new houses!'

'A huge Council estate,' supplemented Meg, and there was no mistaking the satisfaction in her voice. 'If that isn't retribution then I don't know what is. Juliet, girl, were I in your place I'd be dancing with glee!'

'I won't dance,' Juliet said, 'but I can't find pity in my heart either. I wonder if they're still living there—— Hush! Here comes Mr Godfrey!'

'The farmer? Speak to him; I'm dying to see what happens!'

The man had aged, but not too much; he came along and Juliet smilingly stepped forward, saying politely,

'Excuse me, but can you tell me whether the Lowthers still live at the Grange?' She stood still in front of him, aware that Meg was also watching his face intently. No sign of recognition, but a tiny frown appeared upon his brow.

'Aye, sure they do.' He thumbed towards the wooded rise upon which the house stood. 'You'd be visiting them?'

'Not today. I just wanted to know if they were still there. Such considerable changes have taken place since I was last in this village.'

'When would that be?' He was slightly puzzled as he looked at her; she had the impression that he was vexed with himself about something he could not for the moment recall.

'Oh,' returned Juliet carelessly, 'a good many years.'

'There's talk of building a complete new town here,' he said. 'I myself used to have a farm, but I was persuaded to sell out to a syndicate. Robbers, they were! I could have got ten times as much if I'd held on to it for another two or three years.'

'The Lowthers won't like the idea of a new town being built here. Perhaps they too will sell out.'

'They've tried. You see, the Grange's on a hill and no one wants it. Up for sale by auction it was—about six months ago, and it didn't get a single bid. Mind you,' went on Mr Godfrey expansively, 'it's been up for sale several times. Take the entrance, now,' he continued, rubbing his chin, 'that was a lovely sight and no mistake. A long wide avenue of trees. Now, they've had a great lump taken from them, for the new road that goes along by their front. Heavy lorries are now using that road and poor Mr Lowther's a broken man.

His wife's aged about twenty years or more. As you know the Lowthers, though, you'll already be aware of all that's happened?' Again that puzzled look, and the most intense scrutiny that took in her face and forehead, her hair and eyes and her figure.

'I didn't know that they've had so much trouble,' said Juliet, wondering whether or not to enlighten him as to who she was. 'They were very well off, though, so I shouldn't have thought they'd worry too much if their house has been lowered in value.'

'Ah, but a few years ago he lost nearly all his money—unwise investments, it was rumoured here in the village. And so he thought to sell out for a big sum. But his house isn't worth a song, not now that he's got hundreds of houses around it, and a road practically at his front door.'

'It must be a very wide road?'

'Fairly wide, but it winds as well, so it took some off the length of the drive as well as the width.' Mr Godfrey shook his head. 'Aye, it was a sad business altogether, for everyone used to look up to Mr Lowther. Now he's just a nobody.'

'They had a daughter?' Juliet, aware that he was looking most curiously at her, wondered again whether or not to tell him who she was.

'Tanya, yes.' A strange pause, and then, 'I take it, miss, that the Lowthers aren't close friends of yours; if they were then you'd know a little more about them.' There was an unmistakable question in his tone, but Juliet merely replied that the Lowthers were not close friends, but that she had known them once and, as she was in the village, she naturally sought information about them.

'It was a shock to find these changes,' she added, and to her relief he nodded his head and went on to say,

'Their daughter was very beautiful—still is, as a matter of fact. She got married, but she's divorced now, and has come back to live with her parents.'

Juliet said, exchanging glances with her friend,

'They once entertained as their guest a Greek——'

'Aye, they did; I recall that all right. Tanya expected him to marry her, but I reckon he was only playing around. These foreigners aren't to be trusted.' He paused and his mind seemed to wander for a space. 'You haven't said exactly when it was that you knew the Lowthers. Did you ever meet their niece?'

Juliet could almost feel the tenseness that had gripped her friend. She threw her an unconcerned glance and a faint smile touched her lips.

'I did, yes.'

'Nice little thing, wasn't she?'

'Plain, though.'

'Very. But what have looks to do with it?'

'You mean, it's what's underneath that matters?' Meg spoke for the first time, and Mr Godfrey nodded.

'Emily—she asked us to call her Juliet because she liked it better than Emily. Well, Juliet ran away in the end. Did you know about that?'

'I knew she ran away, yes.' Juliet awaited some response, but when he remained silent she added, slowly and with a hint of humour to her voice, 'Did she have some special reason for running away?'

Mr Godfrey hesitated a long while before replying to this.

'She did, yes, miss, but I'd rather not talk about it.'

The two girls exchanged glances; Juliet came very near to disclosing her identity, but for some reason she could not explain she kept silent. And a few minutes later she had thanked the old man and both girls were bidding him goodbye.

'He was puzzled,' declared Meg when eventually they were leaving the village, 'even though he failed to recognize you.'

'It was my voice that puzzled him, but he wasn't aware of this. All he knew was that there was something a little familiar about me.' Juliet turned the car on to the main road and soon the village of West Havington was left behind. 'I daresay it will come to him eventually and he'll say to himself, "That young woman had a voice rather like that of Emily Lowther," and that'll set him thinking.'

'But he'll not come up with the answer, that's for sure.' Meg sat back in the seat, making herself more comfortable. 'You've proved one thing today: you'll never ever be recognized by anyone who knew you before.'

'That's true.'

A small silence followed before Meg said,

'How do you feel about the downfall of those who treated you so badly?'

'I don't know....' with some hesitation. 'To be honest, Meg, I feel almost indifferent, so remote have they become.'

'Were I in your place I'd be delighted that they've been punished.'

Juliet made no immediate response to this; before her eyes rose the dark and handsome face of the Greek who, having come into her life, had in so short a time brought such misery to her.

'Had it been Dorian Coralis who'd been punished,' she said at last, and there was a distinct twist of harshness to her mouth, 'I most certainly would have been delighted.'

'That's understandable.'

'But such a mild form of punishment wouldn't fully

have satisfied me,' added Juliet as if Meg had not spoken. 'I'd like to see him writhing in agony!'

Meg frowned and spoke in faintly troubled tones.

'You sound as if you'd torture him, given the opportunity.'

Swiftly Juliet turned her head.

'Yes,' she said, and her voice was calm now, as calm and casual as if she had been talking about the weather. 'Yes, Meg, given the opportunity, I wouldn't hesitate to torture him.'

CHAPTER FOUR

SPRING was in the air and Juliet had just come in from the garden when Meg, who arrived home from work a little later than her friend, announced that her firm was having its staff dance this year at the Wild Boar Hotel, which was just about the most classy—and costly—hotel in the town.

'Apparently there's going to be a merger with another fashion house,' continued Meg, taking off her coat. 'We're going to be very posh, from what I can gather.'

'You mean that you're no longer going to produce the medium-priced dresses and suits?'

'That's right. We're moving up into the very exclusive class.'

'This other fashion house—is it one of the famous ones?'

'It's certainly one of the famous ones,' said Meg, and went on to mention the name. Juliet whistled and, picking up an expensive, glossy magazine, she flicked through the advertisement pages.

'This is one of their adverts.' She pointed to the picture of two glamorous models who, clothed in exclusive evening gowns, lounged with graceful lassitude against the background of a colonnaded mosque in Turkey. 'That's only a prop, of course,' she added, tapping the amber-coloured backcloth, but even as she spoke Meg was shaking her head.

'No, it isn't. Their backgrounds are all authentic. The models go to Egypt, to pose in front of a pyramid, to Petra to pose in front of some tomb or other. They travel all over the place. I've been learning a lot today about this firm we're merging with.' From her handbag she withdrew two tickets. 'The second of April, so you'd better begin looking for a super evening dress!'

'The Wild Boar,' murmured Juliet, looking at the ticket which Meg had handed to her. 'I shall look forward to this.'

She wore a long dress of apple-green velvet, with tiny bands of deeper green ribbon as trimming for the hem, the neckband, and the sleeves. Her hair shone, newly washed and set, her flawless skin glowed with health, her big brown eyes, shaded by long silken lashes, were clear and bright, revealing the happiness and contentment of their owner. For life was good now for Juliet, and as she entered the hotel there were many eyes that, seeing her, remained fixed upon her lovely face, taking in the evidence that here was a girl whose existence was a joy to her.

And one pair of eyes belonged a tall dark man, a man whose noble bearing and classical good looks had brought many a gasp to feminine lips when, a short while previously, he had made his entrance through the same high wide door as Juliet. She saw him at once, and stood still, the attractive under-film of colour draining from her cheeks. A fluttering hand went automatically to her heart, because it was thudding so violently, causing her pulse to race.

'It can't be!' Still standing as one transfixed, she was denying the evidence of her own eyes. But no.... There was no mistaking that face, those arrogant shoulders, the lithe and muscled frame, towering above the man to whom he was speaking as he stood by the glittering bar, glass in hand.

'Something wrong?' from Meg in a perplexed voice. 'You look as if you've seen a ghost.'

A ghost....

As if suddenly sensing her interest, the man turned his head; Juliet's eyes met his and she saw them open wide. And she almost twisted right round and fled, into the cool fresh air of the garden, away from the man whom she hated with a venom so strong that she could without compunction have seen him tortured, tortured for the untold misery he had caused her when she was little more than a child. But she did not flee, for it was not recognition that made him stare—it could not possibly be recognition. Meg's voice in her ear seemed to calm her a little. She was saying that Juliet had caused quite a stir, over there by the bar.

'That handsome creature's quite unable to take his eyes off you. It could be love at first sight,' she added with a sudden laugh.

Dorian Coralis.... What was he doing here?

His eyes still held hers, held them for a long, long moment before they travelled, slowly and appraisingly, to her lovely neck and shoulders, then down to the tender curves of her breasts and the tiny waistline. The dress flowed in graceful folds down to her feet, and for a few seconds those dark eyes were fixed on the toes of the silver shoes that peeped from beneath the hem.

'We'd better move,' Juliet managed to say, wondering at the steadiness of her voice. 'The cloakroom's over there.'

She and Meg went towards the door and, once inside the room, Meg took off her cape and immediately began to powder her nose, much to Juliet's relief. She had no wish to answer any awkward questions which a puzzled Meg might possibly have asked. Juliet herself, having hung up the black velvet cape, took out a comb and drew it through her hair. Her heart was still beating over-rate, her nerves quivering. Dorian Coralis....

Looking older but as handsome as ever. Maturity had enhanced the dark hair by sprinkling of grey at the temples; his eyes were as keenly discerning as before, his figure just as lithe and lean as when it had first attracted her.

'Are you ready?' Meg picked up her handbag and led the way from the cloakroom. She and Juliet were no sooner in the ballroom than Dorian came over and asked Juliet to dance.

She stepped forward, into his arms, wondering if he could feel the wild pulsation of her heart against him. He held her with a strange gentleness, yet his hold was firm, and warm.

'Tell me your name,' he said when, after dancing half-way round the room, neither he nor Juliet had spoken.

'For what reason?' She looked up as she said this, watching intently for any change of expression in his eyes. There was none; so he had not noticed anything in her voice which could bring back some recollection of the girl whose life he had shattered.

'Must I give a reason?' he inquired with some amusement.

'I'm not in the habit of giving my name to strangers,' she returned, and this made him laugh a little.

'You're being precocious, child.'

Child....

She said,

'I've come a long way since my childhood.'

'How old are you?' The tone was authoritative, masterful. He was sure that he would receive an answer to his question. Her head went up, but Dorian Coralis appeared only to be amused by the action.

'I'm not in the habit of revealing my age to strange men.'

He laughed and swung her almost off her feet as he made for the door into the hotel lounge—the smaller of the three lounges, and the most intimately silent and dimly-lighted. Deep red velvet curtains hung over the windows and the lighting came from beneath the pelmets above them. The reflection was red, rosy red like the carpet and the deep, velvet-covered armchairs. Flowers complemented the soft lights in giving romance to the atmosphere; the soft strains of a waltz drifted seductively on air that was faintly perfumed.

'We shall sit and talk,' stated Dorian, and without more ado he put a hand to her waist and propelled her towards a far corner of the lounge. 'There, my lovely, sit down and tell me about yourself?'

Juliet looked into the dark eyes that she had once hoped would give her a glance of interest and affection. She now saw admiration in their depths, read curiosity ... and desire. So the man's morals had not changed; he was still ready to embark on an affair with a beautiful girl.

If only she could use his desire as an instrument of revenge....

'I find you presumptuous,' she said quietly, 'and also far too confident of yourself.'

Dorian raised his eyebrows; it was plain that this treatment was far from familiar to him.

'Would you care to explain?' he invited, and now his voice held the merest tinge of acidity.

'You bring me in here, tell me to sit down, and almost demand a resumé of my life's history.'

'You made no protest when I brought you in here,' he was swift to remind her. She remained calm, unruffled, her thoughts taking a backward path to the days when she had been naïve, gauche, totally lacking in confidence.

'I am making a protest now,' she began, when he interrupted her with,

'Too late, my child. I have you here, with not a soul in sight, and so you are in my power.'

In spite of herself Juliet found a smile coming to her lips and hovering there. Dorian's eyes flickered strangely as they became fixed on those lips. She knew without any doubt at all that he wanted to kiss her.

She leant back in her chair and crossed her legs. The folds of her dress moulded with her body and his eyes moved. Desire was there—and confidence. Juliet's hatred of him was like a fire ignited from an ember that had withstood the elements of destruction, and the fire was taking hold so that it would consume her whole mind and body.

'Tell me,' she said, 'what is in your mind at this moment?'

At this his lips twitched with amusement.

'Were I to tell you, then you'd either slap my face or wish to know more about the financial aspect of the matter.' Dorian leant back, his dark eyes never leaving her face. Juliet hoped she had not blushed, but rather feared that she had. She lowered her lashes, and thought she heard a slight intake of his breath. Her lashes had always been naturally long and curling; they had made shadows on her cheeks, and in the present subdued light they made shadows that were more alluring than ever.

'You are not English,' she said. 'Are you—Italian?'

'I'm Greek, from the island of Thassos. The name's Dorian Coralis.' He paused a moment, expecting her to say something. 'Aren't you going to tell me your name?' he asked, and his voice had become almost tender. 'What harm can there be in that?'

She looked at him across the table.

'My name's Juliet Hardy.' She waited, holding her breath, suddenly aware that at some time during his visit to the Grange he might just have heard the name Juliet. Still, even if he had, he could not possibly connect the drab little servant girl with the girl he saw before him now.

'Juliet....' The name rolled from his tongue; it was akin to a caress, she thought, and something within her grew and expanded. It was elation, even though she could not have explained just what she had in mind. 'What an enchanting name. As beautiful as its owner,' he added, and his mouth curved in a smile. Juliet caught her breath as she recalled even yet again how she had been attracted to the man, attracted by his smile, his noble carriage, his voice ... everything about him, in fact. 'Juliet, tell me some more about yourself.'

She smiled at him.

'Do you cross-examine every woman you meet?' she inquired with a hint of humour.

'If I'm interested enough,' was his somewhat indirect reply.

'And you are interested in me?'

For a long moment there was silence; a candle on the table flickered in the moving air and the lights in Juliet's hair were flickering too.

'I have never been more interested in a woman in my life,' was his flattering answer at last, and once again his companion's beautiful lashes were lowered. Triumph held her in its grip; her mind grappled for a hint of inspiration as to how she could use this situation in her avid desire for revenge. She had declared she would bring the man to the dust if ever the opportunity arose, and this wish was as strong as ever.

'I suppose I should be flattered, Mr Coralis——'

'Dorian,' he interrupted softly. 'Say it, Juliet. I want to hear it come from those adorable lips of yours.'

She hesitated, for a fleeting moment shy and tongue-tied. But then she murmured, in her gentle, musical voice,

'Dorian....' How many, many times, in those far-off days, had she whispered into her pillow, a pillow damp with tears, 'Dorian ... *please* like me a little.'

He stared at her for a long and silent moment before speaking. Juliet had the extraordinary impression that this confident, self-possessed Greek was at a loss for words.

'It sounds wonderful,' was all he said, and for a while he seemed to be listening to the soft strains of the music—or perhaps he was deep in reflection, she thought, watching his expression closely. 'You and I were destined to meet here tonight,' he murmured at last. 'Little did I know, when I entered on this business project, that I was to meet so beautiful a girl as you. Before this night's out we shall have arranged to meet again.'

'You seem very sure of my acquiescence,' she said tartly, lifting her head as she assumed an air of indignation.

'I believe in fate,' he returned seriously.

Fate.... She dwelt on this, instinctively recalling those days when he had so despised her, and she wondered how he would react were she to tell him that she was the girl whom he had first met at the home of her aunt and uncle, Mr and Mrs Lowther.

'You say you are here on business,' she ventured. 'Did you come all the way from Greece solely for this?'

He nodded his head, and after a moment she was hearing the surprising news that Dorian's father had been the head of the fashion house concerned in the merger of which Meg had spoken.

'But I understood that your father's business was shipping——' She stopped, but too late. Dorian glanced swiftly at her, his eyes opening wide.

'You did?' he murmured, very softly.

'This fashion business,' she began, endeavouring to sidetrack the question in his voice and glance, 'you're here to conduct the merger?'

His dark eyes were curious, his mouth a little tight.

'How did you come to know that my father was in the shipping business?' he inquired, ignoring her query.

Juliet was frowning, angry with herself for the slip.

'I suppose I heard it somewhere,' she replied. 'My friend, Meg, works for the company you're merging with.'

His gaze was still fixed intently upon her; she would have given anything to know what was going on in his mind. From his expression there was nothing at all to be derived; his face was an unemotional mask.

'I see....' No more than this; he rose majestically from the luxurious depths of his chair and held out a hand. 'Let's dance,' he said, and before she quite knew what he was doing she felt her hand taken in a strong firm grip and she was pulled to her feet. A moment later she was in his arms, dancing with him, closely held, and with his head bent so that his lean brown cheek was lightly touching hers. Before the dance was ended his head had moved, so that his lips had found the delicate skin of her temple where it met the hair-line. 'You are adorable!' he told her as he took her back to the spot from where he had approached her in the first place. She coloured daintily and he drew a deep breath.

'My friend's here,' she said, marvelling at the steadiness of her voice. It was certainly not in unison with the beating of her heart!

'Meg?' But he did not wait to be introduced, a circumstance for which she was profoundly grateful, since an introduction would undoubtedly have taken Meg by surprise and she might have made a slip—just as Juliet herself had a few minutes ago.

'You all right?' Meg looked anxiously at her, then turned her head, her eyes following the tall and arrogant figure of Dorian as he strode away. 'He didn't make a pass at you, did he?'

Juliet managed to laugh.

'I believe he did,' was her response, and Meg's eyes lit with amusement.

'I did suggest it might be love at first sight,' was her immediate reminder. 'He just couldn't drag his eyes away from you——'

'Rubbish!' Juliet was still laughing, but within her heart there was tumult. So unexpected a meeting was sufficient for one evening, but to become possessed of the fact that she appealed to the man as well....

'My dearest Juliet,' admonished her friend, taking her arm affectionately and edging her towards the bar, 'your modesty is misplaced. You must know how great your attraction for men is, for we never go anywhere but what you're sought out by aspiring males whom you leave brokenhearted.'

Both girls laughed, and went to the bar where they stood after ordering their drinks.

'That man,' said Juliet quietly, 'is Dorian Coralis.'

'He is?' from Meg without much interest. 'Apparently he's something to do with the merger—— What did you say?' she almost shouted, her eyes becoming like saucers. 'Did you say—*Dorian Coralis*?'

She was shaking her head bewilderedly as she spoke. 'No, it *can't* be the same....' Again she stopped, this time allowing her voice to trail away more slowly. 'It *is* the one, isn't it?'

'The man who caused me all that misery.' Juliet's eyes were hard, and glittering like points of ice. 'Yes, Meg, it is the same man. By some miracle we've met again.'

Meg could only stare, unaware even that the drinks had appeared; and so it was Juliet who opened her dainty, pearl-embroidered evening bag. 'Oh,' she exclaimed. 'I've forgotten my purse!'

'Allow me.' Dorian was there, at her side, and she turned, meeting the admiration and the amusement in his fine dark eyes. 'Aren't you glad I happened to be here?'

'Meg would have paid,' was the ungracious retort.

The money changed hands before Dorian looked once again at Juliet. Collecting herself, Meg glanced at her friend, who immediately introduced her to Dorian. Meg looked up into his face, critically examining him and not caring one jot that he was regarding her with arrogant inquiry.

'How do you do,' she said at last, and a frown came to Dorian's brow and settled there.

'Thank you for paying for our drinks.' Juliet spoke at length, her voice hard and faintly condescending. Dorian's expression was an enigmatical mask, but Juliet sensed his surprise at her attitude towards him.

'It's a pleasure.' Gracious the tone and half-smiling the eyes; Meg glanced at her friend from under her lashes and her lips silently formed the words.

'Love at first sight.'

Could this be so? Juliet asked herself later in the evening when, it seemed, Dorian intended that no one else should dance with her. He had made straight for her each time the music started up, and during the interval he had monopolized her completely. When she went alone to the buffet table—Meg having gone off with a friend of hers—Dorian was soon beside her, wanting to know what he could get for her, and escorting her to a table on the verandah overlooking the gardens of the hotel. It certainly seemed that he intended to carry the acquaintanceship further—much further. And as this was accepted by her she naturally looked ahead to what would ensue as a result of any friendship which he intended to form with her. He had intimated that he was ready for an affair, but if by a miracle it was love he felt for her, then marriage would be his aim, surely? Marriage.... Revenge loomed large on the horizon, since, were she to become his wife, then she could inflict untold misery on him, could bring him to the dust ... the dust at her feet....

Juliet glanced at her reflection in the mirror, picked up her cloak and evening bag, and left the bedroom. Meg was in the hall, talking on the telephone, but she whistled softly as, glancing upwards, she saw her friend descending the stairs.

'You look lovely, Juliet! Have a wonderful time. You know, I think he's marvellous!'

Juliet's mouth curved.

'You keep repeating that,' she reminded Meg. 'You seem to have fallen for his charm.'

'And who wouldn't!'

'I wouldn't, for one.' Juliet's smile was hard, her eyes cold and calculating. 'I'm quite immune, Meg, simply because I'm not the trusting, love-struck child I was when he first knew me.'

Meg spoke into the receiver again, then listened for a moment. She then said goodbye and replaced the receiver on its rest.

'You're not very forgiving,' she said, and Juliet instantly nodded in agreement.

'I'll never forgive him—never!'

'He's in love with you, Juliet.'

'The man doesn't know what love is!' She was angry and bitterly disappointed at the results of her endeavours to extract a proposal of marriage from him. She had had a whole week, seeing him every evening, with full day trips out on Saturday and Sunday, but she was no nearer her aim. It would appear that his feelings for her—whatever they might be—did not go sufficiently deep for him to offer her marriage.

'You'd marry him, wouldn't you—if he asked you?'

Juliet's eyes flickered.

'What reason have you for being so sure? You know that I hate him.'

'And it's because you hate him that you'd marry him.'

'You're very perceptive,' owned Juliet after a small pause. 'Yes, I'd marry him, and make him suffer! I'd crucify him! His love would be his own torture, because I'd throw it in his face.'

Meg was frowning heavily.

'All this is so out of character,' she began. 'I've seen you with children, and with animals; you've a soft heart, Juliet——'

'But not where that man's concerned. He brought me untold heartbreak and humiliation, Meg, and I feel the need for revenge; it's something stronger than I, than my natural inclinations. Don't forget, my hatred's been growing for a long time.'

'It could be your own downfall,' said Meg in

troubled tones. 'Why not forget it—and the man—altogether?'

'It looks as if I shall have to do just that,' returned Juliet. 'He's returning to Greece tomorrow afternoon.'

'He is? Oh, well, I truly believe it's for the best.' A pause, but Juliet made no further comment. 'It's puzzling to me that he's not wanting to marry you....' Meg was pensively looking into space, and talking to herself more than to her friend.

'There's nothing puzzling about it, Meg. He believes he can get all he wants without marriage. He always has, remember.'

'But it's a bit late now for him to be thinking he can get you without marriage.' Another pause and then, 'Has he been trying?'

A smile that was almost a sneer touched the corners of Juliet's mouth.

'Trying his hardest—and getting nowhere.'

'He's given you a marvellous time.'

'And would have done even better. He wanted to buy me a diamond-bracelet, but I refused it.'

'More fool you! It would at least have repaid a little for what he'd done to you in the past.'

'Nothing he could do would ever repay me for the suffering he caused.'

'I agree that he was a hateful creature. But, somehow, I can't help feeling sorry for him now. I know he loves you, Juliet; it's sort of—*instinct*, if you know what I mean?'

Bypassing this, Juliet said, glancing at her watch,

'He should have been here by now.' Perhaps he would not come. He hadn't been at all pleased with her last night when, after the response to his kisses had aroused his ardour, she had coolly pulled herself from his embrace and said it was time he was taking her home.

'He'll be here,' with confidence from Meg. And after a small silence, she repeated, 'He does love you, Juliet.'

'I believe he does feel something rather stronger than desire,' agreed Juliet after some thought. 'But he's obviously not prepared to give up his freedom.'

And Juliet was right. The evening passed off quite well, with a first-class dinner eaten in the luxurious surroundings of a hotel whose dining-room overlooked the river. But although Dorian's expression was one of affection and admiration, his lips never voiced one word about marriage.

'I'd never have believed you to be a prude, Juliet,' he whispered when, after a stroll in the scented woodlands backing the gardens of the hotel, he drew her to him and kissed her, so very tenderly. 'Come, my love, and live on my island. I'll give you everything you want—a pretty villa by the sea, an open cheque for clothes once a month. I'll buy you the loveliest of jewellery.'

'Tempting, but you see, Dorian. I'm not a girl like that.'

'Old-fashioned, eh?'

'You should know that already.' She was still in his arms, and the moon was full in a deep purple sky; the reflection of stars and lights on the river lent its contribution to the romance of the evening. Juliet lifted her eyes to his and he saw the sadness in them. 'Kiss me,' she whispered, and she trembled in his arms, nestling closer as his lips came eagerly to hers. How hard she was trying! Would he not respond—or rather, would he not fling aside his armour and accept defeat?

'I want you, Juliet,' he whispered hoarsely, his mouth in sensuous contact with the curve of her breast, revealed by his deliberate removal of one pretty shoulder strap of the dress she wore. 'I need you! Juliet, you must come to me—you must!'

'Only in marriage,' she murmured, and waited, breathless, for his reaction. He held her from him and she saw that he frowned.

'I'm not the marrying kind,' he said. 'If I were, then believe me, it would be you whom I would choose.'

'Don't you want to settle down—not ever?'

'My freedom's far too precious to me.' Yet his tones were tender, his warm firm hands gentle as if he were handling a new-born baby. 'Dear, dear Juliet, say you'll come back with me to Greece tomorrow.'

She gave a deep and defeated sigh. She had tried, and lost, and there was nothing for it but to say goodbye. She hoped his punishment would come in some other way.

'I said I believed in fate,' he was saying when, a long while after midnight, he was sitting beside her in the car, which was drawn up outside Juliet's front door. 'I can't think that you and I will never meet again.'

'It's unlikely that we shall, Dorian.' She turned to him in the darkness of the car. 'If you loved me, then there would be no difficulty.'

'You'd marry me?' He spoke softly and, it seemed, tenderly. Yet Juliet experienced a strange feeling that he was suspicious of her, distrusting her sincerity. Perhaps, she thought, he was wondering if she were more interested in his wealth than she was in him.

'I'd marry you, Dorian. You already know that.'

Silence. The world was dark around them, but the air was deliciously perfumed by the night-scented stocks which bloomed in Juliet's small front garden. The perfume invaded the car and added to the atmosphere of peace and friendship that, on the surface, lay between the two people sitting there. Dorian seemed not to resent too much her unwillingness to fall in with his desires, while she herself was acting her part so well that there was a self-deceptive element which seemed to hide from her consciousness the fact that she had schemed to trap him in the hope of inflicting punishment on him for the harm he had done her in the past. Had she examined her feelings at this particular time she would have been totally unable to analyse them.

'You'd marry me.' The murmured words came softly, and tender as a summer breeze. 'If I loved you, you'd marry me.' It was not a question, but a statement born of Juliet's own admission. 'But you won't become my pillow friend?'

'If I did,' she returned curiously, 'how far down on the list would I be?'

He frowned when she expected laughter, spoke sharply when she waited for amusement to enter his voice.

'That, my dear Juliet, is the most indelicate question I have ever been asked by a woman. I would not have expected it to come from you.'

'Oh—why?' Intrigued, she was also ready to spar with him. 'It can't be that you consider me too shy to phrase such a question, surely?'

'Not shy, but restrained.'

'I see....' She turned to him again, deliberately allowing her soft cheek to touch his shoulder. 'Well, shall we let that rest? But tell me instead, if you've ever had an Englishwoman for a pillow friend?'

'One or two,' he admitted, his frown deepening.

'Did they live in—er—London?'

'One lived in a small village in Dorset.'

'She did?' Juliet paused, carefully selecting her

words. 'How did you come to be in a small English village?'

'I was visiting some people there. This young woman was their daughter.'

Juliet fell silent, sure that this was as far as Dorian would go regarding his affair with Tanya. Much as she hated him she would not deny him credit for keeping his own counsel concerning his affairs with women. Yet Juliet was curious about his attitude towards herself at that particular time, curious to learn whether or not he was as reticent as he ought to be. She was some time broaching the subject, since it was difficult to do so without giving him cause for suspicion. At length she said,

'The people you visited—they were your friends?'

'Not friends, merely acquaintances I met through their daughter.' Was there an edge of contempt to his voice, she wondered, or had she imagined it?

'They had other children?'

'Not of their own. They had a niece.'

Juliet hesitated; Dorian was frowning impatiently; this she saw indistinctly, but in any case she could sense his impatience with this conversation which he would undoubtedly be considering to be a waste of time. But she was driven on by some force she could not control, driven to ask him about this niece he had mentioned. She inquired about her age, and what she was like.

'She was very young, barely seventeen, and as plain as any girl could be.' He paused a moment and then, 'I'm afraid I don't understand your sudden interest in someone you'll never meet. The girl was a little wanton and had she been a sister of mine I'd have leathered her till she screamed out for mercy.'

Juliet turned swiftly away, aware of her rising colour,

and of the fury that accompanied it.

'It's time I was going in,' she said at length. 'Meg'll not be able to sleep until she knows I'm safely indoors and the bolts are in place.'

'I can't let you go!' He caught her to him and smothered her face and neck with kisses. 'Juliet, give me your answer! I command you to do so!' His lips found hers and crushed them unmercifully. 'I shall not let you escape me!' He was all Greek in this moment, like some supreme god whose word was a law unto itself, whose command could not be disobeyed. Juliet felt, in spite of the cool exterior with which she was attired, the power of him, the mastery and the arrogance. His arms were like bands of steel, his mouth was cruel and demanding, his body possessive in its strength and in its hardness. She lay passive, aware that this kind of lovemaking would please some women—most women, perhaps—but to her it was nauseating, simply because of the hatred she felt for this man. 'Come with me, I say—come with me tomorrow!'

'I must go in,' she said calmly, just as if he had never spoken those passionate and commanding words. 'It's almost half-past twelve.' She had the car door open and, with a shrug of resignation, Dorian slid from his side and walked round to hers. He held the door for her, then reached inside the car to pick up the little evening bag she had dropped, and which she would have forgotten had he not discovered it and given it to her. 'Goodbye, Dorian,' she whispered and, reaching up on tip-toe, she touched his lips with hers. 'Have a safe journey home.'

'Juliet ... we can't part like this....' But she had run along the short path and the fumbling noise she made with the key drowned what he was saying. She entered the hall, and closed the door without turning her head. The engine caught and the purr of the car was heard. And then all was silence in the road outside.

She had lost. That last kiss, given him in one final all-exertive effort to pierce his armour, had failed.

CHAPTER FIVE

It was Meg who brought the message, in a long white envelope which, on entering the house, she handed to her friend.

'From our managing director to you,' she explained, her eyes twinkling as she noted the expression of blank bewilderment that appeared on her friend's face. 'There's a rumour that he was looking for new models and he saw you—at the staff dance——'

'New models,' repeated Juliet, staring at the envelope she held in her hand, and which was addressed to her personally.

'For the ravishing clothes that are being produced now that the merger's taken place. Anyway, open up and let's have a look-see what's going on.'

Judith did as she was requested and was soon reading the letter out loud to her friend.

'Well,' she gasped when she had finished, 'what about that?'

'The chance of a lifetime. You lucky thing! Modelling our beautiful clothes is enough to make me green with envy, but to be invited to go abroad....'

'I'd see the Pyramids, and places like Biblos, perhaps.'

'And the Acropolis of Athens, and the Roman columns and whatnot.'

Juliet made no comment now; she was thinking of Dorian and wondering suddenly if he had had a hand in this.

'I've to see your managing director at five-thirty tomorrow evening,' she said at last. She had already read out this piece of information, but she now added, 'It's a strange time. I mean, the firm closes up at five o'clock.'

'So does yours. And so Mr Boothby's waiting for you. Considerate of him, isn't it?'

'And considerate also to offer to have me trained as a model.' The more she thought about it the more Juliet was convinced that this was Dorian's doing.

She arrived at the office at five-thirty prompt and was shown into Mr Boothby's office by his secretary, who had also waited behind for Juliet's arrival.

'Ah, Miss Hardy.' The big, broad-shouldered man rose as she entered and held out a hand. 'You remember me, I hope?'

She smiled and nodded her head.

'Of course. At the staff dance you spent some considerable time with Mr Coralis who, I believe, is the man behind the merger?'

'That's correct.' He flicked a hand, indicating a chair. 'Do take a seat, Miss Hardy.'

'Thank you.' She sat down and began drawing off her gloves. 'Your letter was a great surprise to me, Mr Boothby.'

'I expect it was.' His appraising glance covered everything from the top of her head to her tiny waist. 'We're looking for beautiful girls—exceedingly beautiful girls, Miss Hardy, to show off to perfection the models which we are now producing. As you know—since it's been in all the newspapers—one of the most famous London fashion houses now controls this company, and in consequence the clothes we shall produce are far superior to those we produced before.'

'They were beautiful, all the same,' Juliet just had to say, because it was the truth.

'We have liked to think so. But now we shall be making clothes for the highest ladies in the land—and for ladies of other countries as well. The gentleman you have mentioned attaches the greatest importance to advertising, hence the order for us to find some really beautiful girls for modelling. As I mentioned in the letter, you will be expected to go abroad.'

Her eyes flickering curiously, Juliet asked,

'Where would I have to go to first, Mr Boothby?'

'Greece.'

'Ah....' Something inside her jerked, causing her pulse to quicken. 'What part of Greece, Mr Boothby?'

'Thassos. We intend to use the extensive archaeological remains there as backgrounds for our models. There are ruins on other islands in the vicinity which, I believe, will also be used.'

'Thassos....' She looked hard at him. 'This offer which you make me is done so at the request of Mr Coralis, I presume?'

The man looked slightly uncomfortable.

'Yes, Miss Hardy. But you are not obliged to accept the post, as you very well know.'

She sat very still, absently fingering the fastening of her handbag. Thassos.... And Dorian Coralis, who had not given up hope, apparently.

'I'll accept the post, Mr Boothby,' she said, and within a fortnight she was being met at the airport at Kavalla by the man she hated most in the whole world. He came towards her, a smile of welcome on his face, his hands outstretched.

'Juliet, so we meet again!'

'I was supposed to undergo some training,' she told him, rather curtly, but she allowed him to take hold of her hands. 'Mr Boothby changed his mind, saying you would see to it at this end.'

Dorian laughed; he looked young, and profoundly happy.

'If you want to train as a model, my dear, then you shall!'

'But you have other ideas about my future?'

'Juliet, my love,' he said chidingly, 'first things first. Enough it is that I have got you here. You've no idea how anxious I've been, telling myself that you wouldn't come.' Possessively he took her arm. 'We have to cross to Thassos by ferry,' he told her. 'There's one due to sail in an hour.'

On the boat he talked about the island, asserting that it was considered by many people to be the most beautiful island in the Aegean. It had been called 'The Circular Paradise', he said, because, in shape, it was round.

'We have tracts of forest and clear crystal streams,' he continued enthusiastically. 'We have many beautiful bathing beaches, some of them idyllically situated. You'll see villages hiding among the mountains. The views are magnificent—you can see the coast and mountains of Thrace when the air is clear, which it nearly always is in summer. And you can see Mount Athos from my house. You'll love my home, Juliet.'

'Your home?' Juliet's flesh tingled. 'Mr Boothby said there would be accommodation booked at an hotel——'

'All full, my love, so you're staying with me.' Quiet the tone but inflexible; Juliet knew that argument would be futile. She would be living in his 'mansion' whether she liked it or not, the home of a millionaire. And he was interested—keenly interested—in someone he had once despised, a girl whose hands, even, seemed to nauseate him. She glanced at her hands when, after landing on the island, they began their drive, in Dorian's Jensen car, from the harbour to his home.

Long slender fingers, almond-shaped nails. Dorian had, during that week they had had together before he left England, often remarked on the smooth, unblemished beauty of her hands.

'Juliet,' he murmured as the port was left behind, 'are you going to let me take care of you?'

'I've come to model clothes, Dorian,' she reminded him, but she looked away, knowing as she did that her one and only object in accepting the post was to attempt once again to extract a proposal of marriage from Dorian.

'You wretch, Juliet,' was his softly-spoken comment. 'I shall spank you in the end, of this I'm absolutely sure.'

'I should immediately go home,' she warned, and Dorian gave a gust of laughter.

'You and I are going to have fun,' he predicted. 'Why, oh, why haven't we met before!'

A silence fell at this; Juliet looked out of the window, taking in the beauty of the landscape—the mountains and the indigo sea, smooth as a pond under the golden haze of the summer sun. Hillsides rose, splendidly clothed with trees—aleppo pines and cypresses, plane and fir trees, and the timeless olive.

'This is a beautiful island,' she said when, after the car had taken a bend in the road, the full panorama of the mountains came before her spellbound gaze. 'You're lucky to be living here permanently.'

'You too shall be living here permanently.'

'I've come to model clothes,' she said again, 'and that's exactly what I intend to do. The job won't last for ever, so I shall be leaving quite soon——'

'Juliet,' he broke in, slowing down the car almost to a standstill, 'just what are you trying to tell me—? No, I'll re-phrase that! What are you asking me?'

She coloured, but turned her head in order to conceal this from him.

'I don't know what you mean?' she prevaricated, and received an impatient sigh for her trouble.

'When I get you to my home,' he almost snapped, 'I shall be able to deal more effectively with you!'

'Deal?' she protested. 'That's an ominous word to use!'

'I'm glad you appreciate that. My intentions are to coerce you into submission.'

She looked sideways at him, seeing the firm and rigid line of the jaw, the classical shape of the nose and chin. Undoubtedly he was like a god, she thought, and a flutter of memory brought back the time when she had almost worshipped the man. She continued to stare at his profile, waiting for him to turn his head; this he did and she noted, without surprise, that his dark eyes held a glimmer of amusement. The man could be attractive! When he looked like this, with just that particular expression on his handsome face, he must undoubtedly appeal to any woman who happened to see him—any woman except herself, that was. For her he would never have any appeal; her childhood 'crush' was of the far and distant past, a past that lay shrouded in a mist of unpleasant memories, not least of which was the treatment she had received from Dorian—the treatment and its consequences.

As Meg had said, those relatives who had treated her so badly had been rewarded; it remained only for Dorian Coralis to be rewarded ... in the way she alone could reward him. But first she must become his wife, and seeing that he had gone so far as to bring her here, to his island home, it seemed that Juliet had room for optimism. True, he fully intended to attempt to charm her into accepting another, far different position in his scheme of things, but he was doomed to failure.

They were travelling along a coast road, with the sea shining like crystal glass, and gay fishing boats and caiques serenely lying at anchor, or drifting lazily against the opaline rim of the distant horizon. The sun's rays were brilliant, and hot, quivering against the moutainsides where the green, luxuriant vegetation basked in the silent stillness of the scented air.

At length Dorian turned the car, nosing it into the narrow dusty lane which led to his home. It came into view after a few minutes' climbing had brought the car to another bend; Juliet's eyes widened and she could not suppress the little gasp of appreciation that rose to her lips.

'Like it?' He seemed pleased by her manner. 'Your home, Juliet, if you will only say the word.'

'My home?' She sent him a slanting glance. 'Do you normally have your women friends living in your house?'

'Don't talk like that!' he almost snapped. 'Anyone would think I'd had dozens of women!'

'And haven't you?'

He made no reply and she knew that she had angered him. But she was not unduly troubled, since she could foresee many occasions when she would anger him.

'Here we are.' The car ground to a halt and he jumped out, coming round to her side and opening the door for her before she could do so herself. 'Welcome to Massalia.'

She entered the lovely white hall, turning her head this way and that in her appreciation of tasteful furnishings and drapes, of flowers and colour and paintings on the walls, of expensive bric-à-brac mellowed by time.

'You collect antiques,' she murmured. 'I have a few rather attractive items myself.'

'You have?' He seemed pleased that she was showing interest. 'These here were my father's, but I've collected some items of furniture and silver myself in recent years.' Taking her arm, he led her into the living-room, and at that moment a brown-faced man appeared from somewhere at the far end of the hall.

'I did not hear you come,' he apologized. 'Astero will be here in one moment.'

'Meet Miss Juliet,' smiled Dorian. 'Juliet, Kleanthes. He and his wife and daughter take care of things for me.' He glanced towards a door that had opened. 'Here is Astero, Kleanthes' wife—ah, and here is Kassiana, their daughter.' The two women smiled broadly, and Astero murmured,

'How do you do?—*pos iste?*' while her daughter merely stood shyly to one side, eyeing Juliet up from the toes of pretty sandals to the shining glory of her hair. Juliet smiled and said,

'I'm happy to meet you all.'

'Kleanthes, you can take Miss Juliet's suitcases from the car and put them into her room.'

'There never was any question of my staying at an hotel, was there?' Juliet was asking some time later as she and Dorian sat on the patio drinking iced lemonade made with fruit from Dorian's own orchard. He laughed and shook his head. And then he added, 'There wasn't any question of your becoming a model, either.'

Silence. Juliet's fingers tightened around the glass she held.

'Then why,' she inquired coldly, 'am I here——?'

'Don't keep up this ridiculous pretence,' he broke in impatiently. 'You knew full well when you accepted that offer that my hand had been at work to bring about your coming to Thassos.'

'I knew that you were the man who had offered me the post, yes.'

'You also knew what I wanted.'

'I knew also what *I* wanted,' she said, but silently. Aloud she told him in no uncertain terms that if she was not to be employed as a model then she would be returning to England at the earliest possible time.

'I told you when we were in England that I would never become your pillow friend,' she reminded him, 'and I meant it.' She had coloured slightly and Dorian, watching her closely, shook his head in a gesture that could have indicated defeat. However, he began to use his persuasive powers and as she listened, she did wonder just how much her cousin had made out of this man who was once her lover. For his generosity seemed to be unbounded and Juliet had to admit that nine women out of ten would be tempted. Dorian was offering a villa, fully furnished, a car, clothes, jewellery.

'But, my sweet, with you I am desiring that you will live at first in my house, since it has long needed a beautiful mistress like you. If the time ever comes when either of us wish to part, then you will have your own villa, which you can occupy or sell, just as you wish.'

She listened quietly, her hands clasped in her lap, until he had finished speaking. And then she looked directly at him and said,

'Dorian, it's marriage or nothing.'

He held his silence for a space and then,

'You're proposing to me? You were doing so in the car as we came along.'

Juliet's colour deepened ... and so did the admiration in her companion's eyes.

'That's not very nice of you,' she told him. 'I would never dream of asking a man to marry me.'

'But you've just done exactly that.'

She shook her head, and a frown touched the lovely line of her forehead.

'Perhaps we should change the subject, Dorian.'

'No, this thing has to be thrashed out—now!'

'If you cared sufficiently,' she said almost in a whisper, 'then you'd want me for your wife.' She looked out pensively to the garden, and to the place where masses of pink bougainvillaea spilled wildly over the walls enclosing part of the shrubbery. Her face was half in shadow, a shadow created by the thick vine which roofed the patio, but the sun's rays were catching her hair, highlighting its glorious colour and its sheen.

Dorian stirred and a slight puckering of his forehead betrayed the fact that he was deeply affected by the situation ... and by the lovely picture of the girl before him.

'If I cared sufficiently....' he repeated after a long while, and it was as if he suddenly realized that a blank page existed in his book of knowledge about women. And that blank page was love. 'Just how much do I care?' This question was not meant for Juliet's ears; she guessed this at once. But she caught the words nevertheless, and she waited, breathlessly, for him to analyse his feelings towards her.

But it was not until much later that day that she received the question for which she had schemed. She and Dorian had taken dinner by candlelight, with the table shining with silver and glass and beautiful crockery. Flowers added colour, and from the tape recorder discreetly tucked away behind one of the drapes, seductive music floated on the air. After dinner they sat on the patio and drank coffee and liqueurs; the full moon spread its light on the mountains and the foothills and sprinkled the crystalline sea with lambent silver which mingled with the starlight and the cloud shadows to form a tapestry of spangled light and shade. Cicadas chirped in the olive trees and from afar a lonely donkey brayed. Juliet, tensed and alert, was beginning to wonder if she were in any real danger from Dorian, as there was no knowing how soon the man's restraint would give way, He was a Greek, and his race was known to be the most amorous in the world; that he was passionate she already had learned, having been bruised by his kisses on more than one occasion. And now, here she was, in his house—and at his mercy. She had known that there might be risks involved, but Mr Boothby's assurance that an hotel would be found for her had completely allayed any fears she might otherwise have experienced.

But her anxieties were not to last for long; no sooner had they finished their drinks than he said, an edge of abruptness to his voice,

'Come, we shall walk, my Juliet—and talk!'

But no talking took place during the first few minutes; once the lights of the house were left behind Dorian stopped beneath a tree, and, taking her in his arms, he kissed her passionately on the lips.

'Dorian—you're hurting me!' The protest was voiced when at length she was allowed a breathing space. 'You're crushing me——' She managed to get that far but no farther. Dorian took possession of her mouth, his own sensuous lips arrogantly demonstrating his mastery over her. She trembled in his arms and was about to make some attempt to break away when he said, his voice hoarse and yet vibrant, betraying the ardour that strove for release,

'Juliet ... you once told me that you'd marry me.

Will you marry me, my love?' His lips were close to her face; she felt his cool clean breath against her cheek.

'You love me?' she asked, even though she knew the question to be unnecessary.

'I adore you! My own, dearest love—say you'll marry me!'

'I'll marry you, Dorian,' she whispered, triumph soaring like a wild bird set forth from a cage. Revenge! The word spread in glaring capitals across her horizon; it filled the sky above her; it was all around her. She would bring this man to the dust!

The wedding had been a grand affair, with many of Dorian's friends present, congratulating him on the beauty of the girl he had chosen for his wife. As for the women present—some were delighted that at last Dorian had landed himself in the marriage net, but there were others who looked with envy on the lovely face of the bride. Arrayed in white, in a long flowing dress of lace with a heavy satin underskirt and several net skirts beneath this, she was a picture of perfection and purity. Dorian's face was a study of pride and love, as, the ceremony over, he walked the length of the church with his bride on his arm.

For Juliet, it was a day of sheer triumph in every way ... yet her thoughts would persist in taking the path she wanted to forget, and she would be in the woods with Dorian, floundering and blundering in her efforts to make him take notice of her. She had loved him then, with a pure and simple love, the love of the child who has reached the brink over which womanhood loomed ahead. She recalled his kisses, his arms about her thin, immature body, a body clothed in garments too big for her, drab, patched garments which caused her many a tearful moment, and many a humiliating hour. Dorian, to whom she had given the abundance of love newly-found, had despised her, looked at her with unmitigated contempt, had 'reported' her to her guardians, had even recommended a beating. She had been plain—almost ugly—and Tanya had been beautiful....

The reception came to an end at last and Juliet found herself alone with her husband. He looked at her long and hard, his eyes dark with adoration and desire.

'What a good day's work that was!' he exclaimed, taking her into his arms. 'I've never done a better in my life—and I never shall!' Words that every bride would have loved to hear, thought Juliet, and for the first time she experienced a tinge of regret. For to every girl her bridegroom's flattery is like nectar and ambrosia mixed together. However, her regret was only momentary, since she had her desire, which was all that mattered, or ever would matter. 'Juliet, my beloved, I shall worship you till I die; this pledge I make you, on this, our wedding day.' Gentle, tender words, spoken with deep sincerity, and he bent his dark head and kissed her with a tenderness he had never shown to a woman before. 'When I think of it now,' he added with a slight frown, 'I cannot conceive how I could have wanted you in any other capacity than as my wife, a wife I will love and cherish forever, a wife who will share my joys—and my sorrows, should there be any.' He held her from him and looked with tender emotion into her eyes. 'Say you love me, my sweet. I don't hear those words very often from these lovely lips of yours.'

She said softly,

'I love you, Dorian.' And then she drew away, biting her lip. Untruths were abhorrent to her, and she had never told them unless it had been necessary in order to save someone trouble or anxiety.

'Tomorrow we shall go on our trip—island-hopping! You'll have a honeymoon to remember, this I promise you!'

They were staying at the villa tonight and tomorrow were embarking on a cruise aboard Dorian's beautiful yacht, *Nereus*.

'I shall look forward to that, Dorian.' She injected a troubled note into her voice and Dorian said anxiously,

'Are you all right, my love?'

She looked up into his eyes and murmured apologetically,

'The day's been far too exciting for me; I feel totally drained.'

He frowned a little.

'You'll be all right soon....'

'Dorian, would you mind very much if I—I—slept on my own for tonight?'

His face registered a sort of dismay, but no anger touched the noble outline of his features.

'If this is what you want, Juliet, but——'

'How good you are! Dear Dorian, I'm very grateful to you!'

The beginning of the torture, she was saying when, half an hour later, she was standing by the bed—the big double bed—listening to her husband moving about in the next room. The door between his apartment and hers was closed, and locked—by Juliet's hand.

Yes, the beginning of the torture. Dorian was in love—deeply in love—with her, so she could make him suffer the pangs of hurt and humiliation which he so richly deserved. How long she could keep his ardour at bay was a question that had, naturally, occurred to her. But she had the answer ready when the day arrived for him to protest. Yes, she had the answer—

the answer that would prove to be the culmination of her revenge....

The lovely white yacht stood at the pierhead, against a background of small caiques and other pleasure craft of the same type as *Nereus,* but smaller. Once aboard, Juliet and Dorian stood on the deck watching Elias, a member of the crew, as he busied himself with ropes and at the same time called out orders to another member of the crew.

'Well, my love——' Dorian turned to his wife and slipped an arm about her shoulders. 'The beginning of a wonderful life together. And the sun shining from a clear blue sky—shining just for you and me.' Tender his accents and low. His expression was tender also, and the touch of his hand as it caressed her bare arm was as gentle as the breath of a midsummer breeze. Despite herself Juliet was affected by the sheer magic of the whole scene and situation—and another pang of regret was felt. What bliss it all could have been were she in love with her husband! A honeymoon to remember, her husband had promised, and undoubtedly it could have been just that. As things were, for Dorian it would prove to be a honeymoon that he would strive to forget, since it would be a mockery, a farce from start to finish.

Their first visit was to the enchanting island of Samothrace, Dorian pointing out to her 'the mountain of the moon' long before the yacht was moored.

'I planned to visit the Sanctuary,' Dorian told her, and this suited Juliet, who had always been interested in the culture of ancient Greece since the day she had set eyes on the snapshot of Dorian which was shown to her by her cousin.

'That'll be lovely!' She must sound loving and affectionate, she had decided, for she desired that the punishment should be so gradual that he would at first fail to recognize that anything was wrong. Juliet planned that disappointment should precede the ache, and the ache should precede the actual pain.

'I'm sure you'll enjoy it.'

'Have you been to all these places already?'

Dorian shook his head.

'Business has hitherto absorbed much of my time, Juliet. But now I shall take time off, since I'm not intending to neglect my wife.' His face wore the expression of a happy man and Juliet's sensation of triumph was heightened. The happier he was at this moment the more desolate he would be later on.

The valley in which the Sanctuary lay was one that had been cut by streams which were now dry, with hillsides clothed with olive trees and cypresses, while high above was the wall of the old city of Samothrace, gleaming and mellow in the sunlight. After exploring the ancient ruins of the temples and other buildings, Juliet and Dorian stood to admire the actual setting of the site.

'All this——' Juliet swept a hand to embrace the whole splendid scene—'for the gods!'

'We were pagans,' he laughed. 'Naturally we gave our gods the very best.'

'I believe that the famous Winged Victory was found on this particular island,' she said, and Dorian immediately congratulated her on her reading.

'That's correct. A Frenchman found it, unfortunately, and sent it to his own country. It's now in the Louvre.'

'Beautifully exhibited,' she added, and Dorian had to agree about this. 'Nevertheless,' went on Juliet with a hint of regret in her voice, 'so lovely and famous a statue ought to be in its own country.'

'I'm glad you think so. However, like so many other important archaeological finds, it rests a long way from home.'

'I don't know why the Greeks allowed people to steal their treasures.'

'Well, people like Elgin and the rest seemed able to do just as they liked, at that particular time. Now, however, no one can take our treasures.'

'Can we climb that hill?' she wanted to know when at last Dorian suggested they leave the the Sanctuary. 'I'd like to sit where Poseidon sat when he watched the Trojan War.' She was laughing and Dorian caught his breath. He seemed unable to speak for a brief space, so deeply was he absorbed by the lovely girl who was his bride.

'You certainly have been doing your homework!' he exclaimed at last. 'Where and when did you read all this?'

'The books came from the library, mainly.' The second part of the question having been answered she paused a while, thinking of those far off days when she had become interested in the Greeks—their people and their country, their ancient heritage of gods and heroes. 'I think I started to be interested when I was about sixteen and a half....'

He looked at her strangely, because of the way in which she had allowed her voice to trail off to silence.

'Tell me,' he said, 'where were you at the age of sixteen and a half?' She shrugged and flicked a hand, indicating that he would not find her answer very interesting. 'I know so little about you, Juliet. We got married so quickly, didn't we?'

'Three days after I arrived here.'

'Three days,' he repeated. 'In all, we've had about a

fortnight in each other's company.' He paused a moment, lost in reflection. 'It will be fun getting to know one another, my love.' They were strolling away from the Sanctuary, his arm about her slender waist. 'Do you really want to climb up there?'

'I'd very much like to do so.'

'As you wish,' he said gallantly. 'This is your day!'

It was not until they had climbed the central peak and were looking out over to Mount Athos that Dorian re-introduced the subject of Juliet's girlhood, asking again where she was at the age of sixteen and a half.

'I was at home, helping with the chores,' she answered when at length she realized that there was no possibility of evading the issue.

'With your parents.' It was not a question as such; Dorian appeared to be taking for granted that it was her parents with whom she lived. 'So you didn't go out to work—not at that time?'

'No, not at that time. I did later, though. I trained for secretarial work.'

'You should have trained to be a model.'

'You think so?' Amusement touched the outline of her lips; she was carried in imagination to what he would say were she to tell him that, at the time in question, she was plain little Emily Lowther, nondescript and not very well educated. 'I rather think I would have been a total failure at that particular time.'

'Nonsense! You must have been an adorably beautiful girl, and an intelligent one!' He paused, but she made no comment. 'Do you not have a photograph?' he asked at length.

'Somewhere—I think.' She had the one he himself had taken, the one she had shown to Meg.

'You think?' with a lift of his brows. 'You must know whether or not you have a photograph of yourself when you were young.'

'If I have it's at home.'

'At home?' with another lift of his eyebrows.

'In England, I mean. I still have many belongings there.'

'Then you must get them over here.' He had already learned a few minor details of her life through little scraps of information she had guardedly let him have. He believed that the couple whose house she had inherited were her parents. Not that she had deliberately lied about them, but she had phrased her information in such a way as to give him the impression that they were in fact her parents. She could not tell him that she had lived with her aunt and uncle—because he might have probed further, in which case she would have found herself in difficulty.

'I still have my house,' she told him. 'I suppose I ought to sell it—or perhaps I shall let it,' she amended, as the idea of a separation entered her mind. For it was doubtful if life with Dorian would continue indefinitely, once she had vented the full weight of her revenge on him.

CHAPTER SIX

THE next island they visited was Lesbos, and then they sailed the smooth blue waters towards the island of Andros, and still Juliet had managed to fob her husband off. She did not feel at all herself; she was all nerves. She was afraid; he must give her time.

'Juliet,' he said in some exasperation, 'what's the matter with you? You're an intelligent, sensible girl who knows what it's all about——'

'Of course, Dorian,' she broke in, a catch in her voice, 'but marriage is—well, it's a complete change from the single life——'

'You knew it would be a change!'

'I think you're most unkind.'

'Do you love me?' he demanded.

'You know I do.'

He bit his lip and she could have laughed. She had him in the palm of her hand . . . and she meant to keep him there.

'Darling, let me show you. . . . I'll be so gentle, so tender. My beloved, I need you so.'

At this she came and put her arms around his neck, and touched his cheek with hers.

'Am I hurting you, dearest Dorian?' she whispered, inserting another catch into her voice. 'I don't want to hurt you.'

He kissed her tenderly before holding her from him and looking deeply into her beautiful eyes.

'Yes, Juliet, you are hurting me—No, that's not quite true,' he amended. 'I'm disappointed, as you must realize. I wanted this honeymoon to be one hundred per cent perfect, one we'd both love to recall over and over again, even when we grow old. But it's being spoiled, for already we've been away for four days.'

'If you'll only be patient for a little while longer, Dorian,' she pleaded in a low tone, 'then all will be wonderful between us.'

'Patient? For how much longer?'

She turned from him and said,

'Is that all you married me for?'

An astounded silence followed.

'It was one of the things I married you for,' he replied frankly. 'It's not unusual, you know, for a man to want to make love to his wife—especially when that wife happens to be his bride!'

'We've all our lives before us——'

'But we can have no substitute for this honeymoon,' he interrupted, and there was no mistaking the tone of deep regret in his voice. 'I've done everything I can to make it perfect——'

'Except have a little patience,' she stated unreasonably.

'Patience! I've already asked you—how much longer must I have patience?'

She put her face in her hands and allowed her shoulders to shake. Within seconds her husband's loving arms were about her and he was asking her forgiveness.

'Darling Juliet, I'm so sorry. But you see, dearest, this is something I just cannot understand.'

'Only because the women you've had were—were. . . .' She could not phrase any more words and he finished for her,

'Wantons, I suppose. And you're so innocent and pure. What a brute I am—totally lacking in understanding. Forgive me, my beloved.'

'Of course I forgive you. Oh, Dorian, please hold me close, and kiss me.'

For a long while he held her, tenderly, protectively, and within her was the hatred she had for him, and the triumph of her present position. How soft and pliable he was!

It was only later that she was to realize just how little she knew her husband, that she was to learn of the traits he had inherited from his pagan ancestors.

They had crossed from the island of Mykonos to the uninhabited island of Delos, birthplace of the twins Apollo and Artemis, whose mother, Leto, being pursued by the serpent Python, was given sanctuary on the island, which was caught by Poseidon and anchored with a diamond pillar. And so Artemis and her brother were born in the safety of the island and Delos later became so sacred to the Greeks that no one was allowed to die or be born there.

Dorian's yacht was left at Mykonos and he and his wife were taken to Delos by caique, landing in a little cove, because the *meltemi*— the 'wind of the islands— was blowing hard, lashing the sea around the islands. Immediately on landing they were among the ruins— fallen columns and other parts of the sacred temples which had been erected to honour the golden sun-god, Apollo, whose cult was as important here as at Delphi where, later, he slew the Python who so relentlessly harassed his mother, Leto.

Juliet was enchanted, and for a while she forgot completely her mission and became the glowing bride that her troubled husband wished her to be. He responded to the change in her, becoming eager and enthusiastic when she wanted to stroll farther afield, or to climb Mount Cynthus in order to gain a clearer view of the neighbouring islands of Mykonos and Rhenae.

'Oh, Dorian,' she sighed when at last she agreed to sit down. 'I've loved every moment of it!'

'So have I.' His glance was one of tender emotion; she saw that he was touched by the change in her and for one fleeting moment her resolve weakened and she felt she could not bring herself to inflict pain upon him. But memory with its cruel barbs descended ruthlessly once more and she herself was suffering the agonies of pain and humiliation, the uncertainties and terrors of being homeless and with scarcely any money in her purse; she recalled the moment of waking up in hospital and the horror of being told that her face was gravely disfigured. She reflected on those long weary months when the plastic surgery was being done, bit by bit until, after several operations, the surgeon was at last satisfied with his handiwork. No relative visited her during that seemingly endless period; no flowers came to her as they did to other patients, no fruit or chocolates or books—other than those passed on to her in kindly gestures from other patients, or from compassionate relations of theirs who, seeing the young girl lying there alone, had decided to afford her a little attention.

'Shall we go now?' he was asking, breaking into her reflections. 'The sea's becoming rougher and rougher with every minute that passes.'

'All right.' She put her hand into the lean brown one that was extended to her, and she came to her feet close to her husband; his finger caught in her chin as she would have bent her head.

'I love you, Juliet,' he whispered, his dark eyes looking tenderly into hers. 'Dearest, let us be happy. Let us begin our real honeymoon tonight.'

She drew away, stiffening slightly, and she noticed

the sudden change of colour in his face. The tan seemed to gain a tinge of grey, especially along the sides of his mouth. His eyes lost their tenderness, his mouth went tight.

'I'm not ready,' she said. 'You'll have to be patient a little while longer.'

She received no response to this, and as they walked back along the famous Terrace of Lions she glanced sideways at him, frowning at his taut and austere profile. Here was a hardness she had never seen before, a ruthlessness that troubled her in a way she failed to understand. She had him in the palm of her hand, she had told herself; he was soft and pliable and, therefore, would give her no trouble. His love for her was strong and deep, and all he desired to do at present was to please her, to pander to her every whim. Of course, the time would arrive when a showdown was inevitable, but surely that time was not yet. And even when it did arrive, it would be she who would inflict the hurt, who would stand back and laugh in his face.

The caique was waiting and they boarded it in silence. The rough sea frightened Juliet, tossing the small boat about as it did, but she could not put out a hand to take that of her husband, or look imploringly at him, asking for his tender, reassuring words.

And quite suddenly she knew that she was losing something.

She stood in the middle of her cabin, clad in a flowing nightdress of layers and layers of flimsy nylon and lace. The neckline was low both back and front, the folds clung seductively to the beautiful contours of her body. She turned to gaze into the long mirror—and she liked what she saw. Fortune had smiled upon her that day when she had been knocked down by the bus

—although she did not think so at the time. So plain she had been, believing that it was the bone structure that was at fault; but the surgeon had told her that her bone structure was perfect, so he had been able to give her beauty far surpassing that of her cousin, whose looks she had so often envied.

Juliet's musings came to an abrupt end as the cabin door swung inwards and her husband stood there, clad in a black and green dressing-gown, the girdle of which was held between his fingers, in much the same manner as Greek men handled their *komboli* as they automatically flicked the beads from one end of the string to the other.

'Do you want something?' she inquired imperturbably.

For answer he came forward a step ... and the cabin door clicked behind him, causing Juliet to give a little start. His dark eyes took in the lovely contours of her body, seductively revealed owing to the diaphanous nature of the material of which her nightdress was made. She shrank into herself, aware of a tingling of nerves, and that the fine gold hairs on her forearms were standing up, away from her flesh. Her question was repeated, and she marvelled at the calm inflection of her voice.

'Want something?' he said, the grey tinge at the corners of his mouth deepening. 'I believe that the first thing I want to do is talk, but I'm not sure.'

Not sure? How unlike her husband to falter like this. Juliet had difficulty in keeping from her gaze all the hatred she felt for him—and the satisfaction that his present attitude afforded her.

'It's rather late for chatting,' she said to him, and noted the hint of a frown that appeared on his low and noble brow.

'It's not a chat I've come for, Juliet....' He came towards her with another step, and he held out his hands to her. 'My Juliet,' he murmured, 'I love you so. I must have all your love, my dearest.' His eyes pleaded and his outstretched arms beseeched. 'Come, sit with me, my love, and let us talk this whole thing out.'

But Juliet shook her head. Inside, she knew disappointment, since it seemed likely that the showdown was to come far more quickly than she had planned. That plan had involved a slow torture where Dorian, patiently awaiting the disappearance of her inhibitions, would lie in his room night after night, brooding and licking a small wound that, very gradually, would widen and fester until eventually it crucified him with pain. For, very slowly, it would come to him that his wife did not love him, had never loved him. Only then would the showdown come—or so this was what Juliet had thought—and she would have her answer ready, the answer that would strip him of both his arrogance and his self-esteem.

She would inform him that she had married him for his money.

'I'm not ready to be your wife, Dorian,' she said at last. 'I've already told you this.' Would he leave her, going to his room to lie awake and wonder just what had gone wrong with his marriage?

But he made no move to go; instead, he sat down on a chair, his eyes fixed on her face in an intense and searching scrutiny. And as she watched, his whole expression changed, and she knew a most uncomfortable trembling deep within her. For there was a distinct hint of brutality in his dark eyes, in the taut line of his jaw, in the thin tight line of his mouth. His nostrils seemed to quiver ... like those of a wild animal on the scenting of its prey.

'Just when will you be ready to be my wife, Juliet?' he inquired in a dangerously quiet tone. 'We've been married for a week now.'

She shrugged, adopting a careless manner she was far from feeling.

'A week's no time at all, Dorian,' she said in tones of protest not unmingled with censure. 'I'm not the first bride to have difficulty.'

'True,' he agreed in that same soft tone, 'but I'll wager you're the first to be so damned unconcerned about it.'

Her eyes opened very wide.

'There's no need to swear,' she admonished. 'And as for being unconcerned—what good will it do me to weep over my shortcomings?'

'Shortcomings, eh?' he repeated grimly. 'So you admit to having shortcomings?'

'I'm honest enough to own that my—er—reluctance is not normal.' And then she spoke softly to him, and tenderly, hoping that she could fob him off for a little while longer, just for the satisfaction of making him suffer the slow agony she had planned for him. 'Darling Dorian, please try to understand. It's so difficult for me, especially as I love you so——'

'Love?' He repeated the word, and it seemed to come from somewhere deep in the centre of his heart. 'Juliet—my dear sweet wife, do you mean that? Say it again, and let me look right into your eyes ... for I wonder now if you really do love me.'

So he was suffering! She looked into his eyes, saw the darkness of misery in them, the shadows of hope slowly dying. Exultation swept through her whole body like a warm and pleasant wave that comes inshore to caress the golden sands. She spoke, but for some reason she could not face the challenge of his gaze, as he had begged her to.

'I love you, dear Dorian. Just be a little more patient....'

'For how long, Juliet—for how long?'

'Another week, or a month, or even——'

'A year!—two years—ten years!' His control was fast deserting him and Juliet realized all too late that she had not been playing her part very well. Yet she should have done; she had rehearsed it often enough!

'Don't be angry with me,' she begged. 'I'm unhappy enough as it is.' She held her breath, for even to her own ears her words had no convincing edge.

'You're unhappy?' Sceptically he looked at her, and suddenly he rose to his feet, his height dominating the cabin, roomy as it was. The arrogance had returned, replacing the shadows of unhappiness in his eyes; the brutality was there, the quivering of his nostrils. 'Do you suppose that you're anywhere near as unhappy as I?'

'Can we assess it—weigh it? Dorian, don't look at me like that! You—you frighten me!'

'Frighten?' Like a miracle his expression underwent another change. 'In what way, Juliet?' He seemed faintly dazed by her assertion and it dawned on her that his brutal qualities were so inherent that he did not know he possessed them.

'You—you're—different.'

He frowned at this.

'In what way different?'

'You look—kind of—of cruel....' She glanced away. For some reason she could not define this deception was becoming most distasteful to her.

Regret and pain entered her husband's eyes. He said in soft and gentle tones,

'Cruel, Juliet?' And he shook his head as if the

idea was hateful to him. 'No, not that, my dear.'

My dear.... She felt safer now, and her courage returned.

'Perhaps I'm mistaken, then. But please, Dorian, leave me now. I really am tired.'

'This is our honeymoon,' he said, and into his voice had crept a hint of anger and impatience. 'Up till now it's been a complete farce.'

That, she thought, was exactly what she had intended it to be.

'You're so impatient——'

'Don't repeat that again,' he broke in wrathfully. 'Impatient? What do you think I'm made of?'

Juliet drew back instinctively till she came against the long heavy drapes. She was conscious of the silence, which seemed to have a suffocating effect on her. She was conscious too of the background noises from without—the sound of waves lapping the sides of the yacht, the strains of music from a *bouzouki* band somewhere in the distance, perhaps on board another luxury vessel moored in the harbour.

'I can't be your wife yet, Dorian——'

'Tell me,' he broke in, and now he was not making any effort to control his swiftly rising fury, 'did you really expect a platonic marriage?'

'Of course not, but——'

'Then what's all this about?' he demanded, moving closer to her. 'You've talked of love, yet you're indifferent even to a caress.' Suddenly he gave a laugh, a harsh and almost demoniacal laugh that echoed through the cabin. 'Love! I'm beginning to doubt that you ever thought of love!'

'Then why would I marry you?' she asked, amazed that she could appear so outwardly cool when, inside, her nerves were rioting.

'That,' he said between his teeth, 'is what I'm intending to find out.' He was very close now, towering above her, his dark eyes boring into her, fixing her gaze. 'Why,' he demanded harshly, '*did* you marry me?'

Juliet was scared by this time and, to make her position worse, she could not gather her thoughts sufficiently to play her part with the effectiveness which she had originally intended. The trouble was that her schemes had gone awry, and this was solely because she had over-estimated her husband's patience and staying power. He was speaking again, repeating his question, but now there were distinct signs in his voice that his fury had reached boiling point.

'We were in love,' she began when he interrupted her.

'Answer my question!' He took her by the shoulders and shook her. 'If you can't see that my patience is exhausted then you're a fool! Answer me, I say!'

'I married you for love——'

'Don't lie!' Again he shook her, his control fast leaving him altogether. 'I can see now that you've been acting a part all along, and you've acted it well, since I was totally taken in!' Cruelly he grasped her chin, jerking it up so that he could look into her eyes. 'But,' he continued harshly, 'the time has come for a full explanation. I demand to know your reason for marrying me!'

She stood, white and trembling and immobile, still imprisoned by the cruel grip of his hands, one on her shoulder, the other keeping its vice-like hold on her chin. A long-drawn-out sigh escaped her as she admitted that the showdown had arrived despite her efforts to postpone it. She had so dreamed of his punishment, of the slow torture of discovering that the wife whom he adored did not love him, had never loved him; for if she had she would never have been able to deny him a physical demonstration of that love. Her plans had gone awry and she felt cheated, felt that all her scheming had been in vain. But no, not quite that, for undoubtedly she had made him suffer. And she could make him suffer more by following her originally intended course—but she resignedly had to admit that the ace she was about to play had lost much of its effect by being prematurely used.

Before she spoke she managed to move, freeing herself from hands that had relaxed their hold. Her own hand went soothingly to her shoulder as, twisting her head, she frowningly espied the grey-blue bruises made by the pressure of his fingertips.

'I married you, Dorian, for your money.'

She did not know quite what she expected, for her mind was still misted and therefore her thoughts were not clear. She had pictured this scene, naturally, and in focusing it she had seen her husband, accepting her explanation, but in so bewildered a way that he would appear as a broken man; she had seen him leave her, to return to his bed where he would toss and turn and nurse his broken heart. And Juliet herself? She would also lie awake, but only to gloat over her triumph for a while before, dismissing her unhappy husband from her mind, she would settle down to sleep the sleep of the just.

Dorian was standing there, staring down at her, his face an inscrutable mask. The clock ticked over on the dressing-table, the only sound intruding into the terrible silence that pervaded the cabin. Suddenly Juliet had an almost hysterical desire to flee from the man before her, the towering Greek whose expression even now was beginning to twist into ugly, satanic lines.

But even were she fully dressed, how could she escape him?

'What did you say?' he asked at last in a very soft tone.

'I think you—you h-heard m-me.' Fear caught her throat and she raised a quivering hand to it. Was he going to murder her? she asked herself, looking wildly about her, as if expecting that by some miracle an avenue of escape would appear.

'For my money....' The dark satanic eyes held depths of smouldering fire. 'Explain a little further, if you please.'

So calm he appeared now ... but Juliet was not deceived. Her husband was consumed by rage.

'Explain?' she faltered. 'I don't know what you mean.'

Dorian looked down at her in silence for a long intimidating moment before he said,

'Am I to take it that you always intended marrying for money—that it did not really matter who might come along?'

She nodded and replied in husky tones that this was correct.

'It just happened to be you,' she added, and was pleased to note that her voice had become a little more steady. She must not allow herself to be browbeaten by this man; such a circumstance held no place in the plans she had so carefully made.

'It just happened to be me....' His accents were slurred; Juliet likened them to the throaty groan of a wild creature about to spring upon some helpless and unsuspecting prey. 'You were always confident that you could "catch" a wealthy man.' A statement, and Juliet made no comment. In fact, she would have had difficulty in doing so, since her throat seemed blocked by the ball of fear that was rising in it; for her husband's voice, and his demeanour, were threatening, to say the least. 'You've always been aware of your beauty—from a very early age, I suppose?' His dark eyes were narrowed to mere slits now. 'And you intended using that beauty as a weapon to attain your desire.'

She still made no comment and as he did not add anything more a silence fell on the cabin—a long, lingering silence which, giving weight and tenseness to the atmosphere, caused Juliet's flesh to tingle, so oppressed was she by it. 'So these inhibitions are all an act?' he said at last and, without waiting for an answer, he added, regarding her curiously, 'What puzzles me is—just how long did you expect to be able to fob me off?'

She managed to shrug her shoulders in a gesture of indifference which she was far from feeling.

'Does it matter?' Why didn't he leave? She had brought his pride to the dust, had given him more than enough to brood upon——

'No!' The one word struck into her thoughts like the sound of a whiplash. 'No, it doesn't matter—not now....' His eyes burned into her, burned with fury and an all-consuming passion. 'Not now, my beautiful wife!' His dressing-gown slid to the floor and he kicked it to one side; her eyes dilated at the action and, frantically, she made a swift move to dart past him to the door. But she was caught in the circle of his arm and before she even had time to think she was crushed to his body and his sensuous lips possessed hers with all the savage cruelty of his pagan forebears. Juliet's senses seemed numbed as, after her first futile endeavour to resist, she ceased to struggle and accepted what her husband in his unbridled fury inflicted on her. His hard and sinewed frame bruised her delicate flesh, his arms were like bands of steel enveloping her, his mouth explored her lovely tender curves with all the arrogance of the victor. Then all at once his hold slackened and she renewed her struggles. Dorian's laugh filled the cabin.

'Struggle to your heart's content, my Juliet!' he said, taking her chin in a brutal grasp and forcing her to look at him. In this position he kept her for what seemed an eternity, just to let her see who was master. She tried to move, saw the gleam of sheer amusement appear in his eyes as, lowering his head, very slowly as though savouring the expression of fear in her eyes, he claimed her lips again.

Breathless when at last he drew away, she could only lean dizzily against him, aware that her legs were on the point of giving way beneath her. Never had she bargained for anything like this and, from the depths of her heart, she was wishing she had given far more thought to what might be the consequences of her action in marrying Dorian for revenge. 'But you're not struggling,' he said in chiding tones. 'Come, you're not giving in so easily?' His dark eyes glimmered and his lips twitched. His fingers were now almost gentle as they flicked her cheek before drawing a line that circled her shoulder and the alluring curve of her breast. 'I would have expected you to put up a little more fight than this.'

She became consumed by rage; it rose above her fear and, twisting round, she managed to break away. But again his laugh rang out and she saw at once that it was a cat-and-mouse game he was playing with her. Her hand was caught, and crushed within his long sinewed fingers; with an arrogant jerk he had her close to him again. His fingers circled her throat and she thought: 'Is he going to strangle me—strangle me and throw me overboard?' Aloud she said, aware of the tears gathering in her eyes,

'Please go away—get out of my cabin——'

'You're talking to your husband,' he broke in softly. 'It's marriage you wanted, my lovely Juliet, and it's marriage you've got. The stage is mine from this moment on.'

'No! Oh, *please* go away! I don't want——' She broke off and began to cry, thoroughly ashamed of her tears but totally unable to control their flow. 'I don't feel very well.'

He laughed softly.

'You'll feel better in a little while, my love.' And once more she was in his arms, his mouth on hers. She became desperate, panic-stricken, and in consequence her strength returned and she struggled for freedom. 'That's better,' he murmured in tones edged with humour. 'Struggle on; you'll have less strength to resist me later—not that I'd have you surrender meekly,' he laughed, 'on the contrary, the victory will be all the sweeter if I have to crush your resistance first.' A small pause and then he added, as if the thought had come to him as a result of these words, 'Your spirit, my clever scheming wife, will be crushed later, quickly or slowly, depending on whether you are sensible or obstinate.'

Her tears continued to fall and angrily she wiped them away with the back of her hand. Self-pity took possession of her, overriding all other emotions; she forgot that she had asked for this, forgot that she had taken risks without adequate pre-action thinking; she failed utterly to see her husband's side of the situation, and to perceive that he must obviously retaliate, if only to save his pride. No, she knew only this one emotion, self-pity, which soon led to an upsurge of her hatred of Dorian Coralis, the man who had caused Emily Lowther such incalculable misery and fear.

'Get out!' she cried, using her fists to batter at his chest. 'Get out or I'll scream so loud that every boat in the harbour will come to my rescue!'

Another laugh rang out, a laugh with no point to it. Dorian shook his head slowly, from side to side.

'You'll not call out,' he told her, and even as he spoke she experienced a great wave of resignation sweeping over her. There was no escape. 'As I've just said,' her husband continued, 'the stage is mine. It will remain mine until, having decided that the farce has gone on long enough, I ring down the curtain.'

Something final in this brought a strange and indefinable flutter to her heart and made her say,

'When will that be?'

The dark eyes looked long and hard into her face.

'When I've tired of you and desire a change.'

Juliet coloured painfully.

'So I'm—I'm....' She could not continue, and her husband finished for her.

'You're my pillow friend after all. I keep you until I see someone I desire more strongly.' A small pause and then, in accents of harsh deliberation, 'There's only one difference, Juliet. As my pillow friend you'd not only have enjoyed many privileges, but you'd have been generously rewarded. Now, you'll neither enjoy privileges, nor will you leave me with anything more than what you came with.' His hands were on her shoulders and before she knew what was happening she was swung right off her feet and carried across the cabin as if she had been no heavier than a doll. He took her into his own cabin, kicking the door to behind him. Tears flooded her eyes, but Dorian was impervious to her distress as, with the movement of an elbow, he snapped off the light, plunging the cabin into total darkness.

CHAPTER SEVEN

DAWN crept through the curtains, grey and misted and sunless. Turning her head on the pillow, Juliet caught her lip between her teeth until it hurt. Dorian lay there, his low, even breathing in tune with the louder, despairing thuds of Juliet's heart.

Slipping from the bed, she stood there for a long while looking down at the face of the man she hated, and a deluge of bitterness engulfed her. For he it was who slept the sleep of the just, and she it was who had spent the sleepless night. So much for her revenge. What was the best thing to do now? Retreat, accepting the defeat that undoubtedly was hers, or stay and occupy a position of total degradation? The decision was not difficult to reach, since Juliet was not in Tanya's class.

Escape....

In her own cabin, she bathed and dressed, then gathered her toilet necessities from the cabinet above the wash-basin. These she placed in a small suitcase; in a larger one she packed some of her clothes, bitterness taking possession again as she relived that other occasion when, stealthily, she had packed her pitiful belongings and stolen away from the Grange at dead of night, entering a bewildering, terrifying world all alone, and with only sufficient money to buy herself a railway ticket and a bed in some cheap lodging-house. She felt the tears pricking, but it was her heart that cried. What a mess she had made of things; what a wasted effort on her part, trying as she had to repay the Greek for all he had done to her. Far better to have forgotten the past altogether, since it was so far behind her, and since her life had become carefree and happy. Now she had to go back—not to begin again, it was true, for she still had her house, and Meg was still in it, taking good care of it. But she had to re-establish herself as regarded a job; she had to do some explaining to her friends and acquaintances. And what of Meg? What would she think about the whole miserable business? That some embarrassment had to be suffered Juliet was only too ready to acknowledge, but she would far rather return to the old life than remain here as Dorian's vassal—which was all her position would amount to.

'Going somewhere?' Soft the tone and enquiring; she glanced up to see her husband leaning against the door jamb. He had pushed in the door without her hearing him do it. His eyes were moving from her face to the suitcase on the bed.

'I'm leaving you.' Pale but composed, Juliet turned away from the expression of amused triumph that her arrogant husband wore. 'I'm going home ... back to England,' she added, as she noticed his straight black brows shoot up a fraction.

'I think not.'

Juliet swung around to face him.

'You can't keep me with you. This yacht's moored and there's nothing to prevent me from stepping off it. That's exactly what I intend doing.'

Dorian took a couple of steps, bringing him into the cabin.

'I was given to understand that you married me for my money. How much do you think you'll collect if you leave me?'

'I'm no longer interested in your money,' she replied, and her husband's eyebrows shot up again.

'A gold-digger doesn't change overnight. I'd like some

sort of explanation from you.'

She turned again, and drew back the curtains. The sea was smooth, and dulled by the reflection of the grey clouds above. The gay little caiques still splashed their colour and on the waterfront itself men in black jerseys sat mending their fishing-nets. A little brown boy stood watching a man slapping an octopus against the pavement, tenderising it ready for the cooking-pot. And from a white-sailed yacht moored not far from *Nereus* there came the sound of laughter. An ordinary day, with an ordinary beginning....

But for Juliet the day had begun much earlier, with the mastery of her husband making it a day of reckoning ... bitter reckoning. His desire for her had reached a peak of uncontrolled passion; his object had been to subjugate her in the way the majority of Greek wives were subjugated by their husbands. He had succeeded, and now, as he stood there in that arrogant pose, a hint of amusement gleaming in his eyes, Juliet felt that her hatred of him would consume her for the rest of her days. She would never be able to forget that, twice in her life, she had been brought down to the depths of humiliation by this man—the first time being through no fault of her own whatsoever. So it was not unnatural that she had desired revenge, or that she had seized the opportunity when it so unexpectedly arose. She believed that she had him in the palm of her hand, having been deceived by his gentleness, his apparent acceptance of the fact that she could not come to him owing to her inhibitions. It would have been laughable—had it not been so shattering—for the woman was not breathing who could have this dark and arrogant Greek in the palm of her hand.

'I've asked you a question, Juliet.' Dorian was still cool and unperturbed and his dark eyes met hers as she twisted round to face him. She was still pale, but embarrassment filled her whole being and with angry self-discipline she thrust away the memory of her husband's lovemaking.

'I'm not willing to be a—a—proper wife to you,' she managed to say, but she lowered her lashes as she spoke.

'A platonic marriage to a wealthy man. This is what you've always had in mind?'

Put like that it sounded absurd in the extreme, but how could she explain without revealing the whole story and telling him who she really was? This she had never for one moment intended doing, since she was convinced that if he knew she was that plain little Emily Lowther, he would instantly cease to love her. And it was his love which she had intended using for the fulfilment of her scheme; his love for her was to be her strong effective weapon with which she would punish him.

'Dorian,' she said, trying to retain some modicum of dignity and calm, 'words are both useless and unnecessary. Our marriage was a mistake; I want to end it. Please don't argue; I've made up my mind.'

His face remained an unreadable mask, but somehow Juliet sensed in him the presence of several emotions: anger and puzzlement, pain and regret. His next words, spoken sharply, gave evidence of the former of these emotions.

'*You* want to end it! And what about me? You've not been completely honest; there's something you're keeping back. I demand to know what it is.'

'I'm unwilling to enter into any discussion or explanation, Dorian. I'm leaving you, and that's all I have to say——'

'You are not! If I have to keep this vessel at sea for the rest of my life I'll keep you with me!' Moving swiftly, he crossed to her and before she knew it she was crushed against him and her face was roughly jerked so that her lips were his for the taking. His mouth was hard and cruel in its unbridled passion; his hands explored with arrogant mastery the delicate curves of her shoulders and throat, and the alluring softness of her breast. She struggled, but in vain. Dorian was determined to teach her that his was the dominant factor in their relationship.

For the next three weeks he kept the *Nereus* at sea, calling at ports only for supplies. His crew had orders not to speak even one word to their mistress, or to answer her if she should ask any questions of them. When the boat was moored by a jetty she was locked in her cabin; when it was moored a little way out she was allowed her freedom, just as she was when the boat was at sea, sailing between the islands. Juliet fumed, straining at the bonds that held her, but nothing she said or did seemed to have any effect upon her husband. He would be masterful and silently morose in turn, arrogantly possessive or icily remote. Never did he display the merest hint of tenderness, and as time went on the idea began to cross her mind that she had made a mistake in assuming that he had ever loved her. This idea persisted until, in the end, she was totally convinced that his sole reason for marrying her was desire for her body.

Many tears were shed as she came finally to admit that her life was ruined, for it now seemed certain that she must remain with her husband indefinitely, since he had it in his power to keep the yacht at sea for as long as he liked.

'People have made boats their homes, so why shouldn't we?' he had said when one day she had asserted that, as he couldn't go on sailing for ever, she must gain her freedom some time. 'We can live like this for years and years if we wish.'

'We?' She looked at him with hard and angry eyes. 'I don't have any say in the matter at all!'

'That's just as it should be. A Greek wife, knowing her inferior position, bends always to her husband's will.'

Juliet swallowed the saliva which seemed repeatedly to fill her mouth.

'I am not a Greek, Dorian,' she reminded him quietly.

'You're married to a Greek and therefore you'll obey the customs of my country. The sooner you resign yourself to the fact that I'm your master, that my every word is law, the happier you'll be——'

'Don't mention the word happiness to me! How can I be happy in circumstances such as these?'

Her anger set his own alight; his eyes burned like live embers responding to a fan. He leapt to his feet and seized her wrist.

'Whose fault is it that the circumstances are what they are? Well——' He shook her unmercifully, evincing nothing but brutal satisfaction at the sudden flow of tears he saw. 'Well, answer me! *Answer me, I say!*'

Dazed by his rough treatment of her, she had no answer ready; instead, she swayed and would have fallen had he not held on to her.

'Can I lie down?' she asked, and although she would never have owned to it her voice was meek and pleading. 'I don't feel very well. I think it must be the heat.'

She was thrust from him, on to the couch, where she stayed for a long moment, wondering why she felt so faint. True, the shaking had unbalanced her, but by now she should have recovered.

At last he seemed to take in the fact that she was not acting, and, striding over to her, he took her wrist between his fingers. A frown appeared on his face; he said he would fetch her some brandy.

'I don't need it,' she began, but he had gone from the saloon, into the cocktail bar just across the passage.

'Drink it,' he ordered, handing her the glass. 'It'll restore your nerves.'

So he was admitting that he had upset her nerves ... but there was no hint of remorse in his expression.

She took the glass and drank the contents, resigned to the fact that defiance would not take her very far. A month of marriage to this dark unbridled pagan had taught her that the practice of caution could save her a great deal of discomfiture.

'I'm all right now,' she said in answer to the silent question in his eyes. 'But I think I'd like to lie down.'

'Very well.'

A few minutes later, when she glanced through the window of her cabin he was on the sun-deck, relaxing in a chair, his brown body clad only in a pair of shorts. He had a book in his hand, and as she watched he flicked the pages and began to read. Juliet frowned heavily, wondering how he could be so resigned to the life they were leading. On a couple of occasions he had seemed bored to distraction, and she had half expected him to say that he had had enough. On another occasion he had repeated what he had previously mentioned about ringing down the curtain—when he was ready. Juliet had been given hope, but now he seemed quite content with things as they were, content to keep on sailing, spending his time reading or lying on the deck in the sun. True, he spent several hours ashore when the *Nereus* arrived at an island, and Juliet supposed that these excursions relieved his boredom to some extent.

As for her own life—she read too, being grateful for the books and magazines which Dorian bought for her when he went ashore. She wrote letters which she could not post, being reluctant to trust them to Dorian, as they contained the information that she would expect to be returning to England in the not too distant future. This suggested that her marriage had broken up, and the information was intended to warn her friends that she would not expect too many questions when, subsequently, she did arrive back in her own country. The longest letter was to Meg, to whom she confided much of what had transpired.

'I'm a prisoner at this time,' she wrote, her letter being in the form of a serial story, 'for Dorian won't allow me off the yacht. He says he can sail the seas indefinitely, but I'm of the opinion that he is already chafing at the inaction of this life. Also, it's inconceivable that his various business projects can continue without at least some attention from him.' Juliet wrote every day, just for something to do, and she felt sure that when the opportunity for posting Meg's letter did arrive, much of it would be cut out.

One day Juliet heard her husband telling the crew to write home to their wives, informing them that they would be away from home for some considerable time. Juliet gasped inwardly at this, and spoke to Dorian later, when they were alone, having dinner in the luxurious dining-saloon.

'This is ridiculous! We can't stay at sea for ever!'

'No?' His calm and unperturbed manner infuriated her. 'Why not? I'm quite happy.'

'Happy?' she repeated sceptically. 'I don't believe you, Dorian.'

At this he merely shrugged his shoulders and Juliet said again that this could continue for ever.

'It will continue until I receive the information for which I am waiting—and which I expect will not be too long in being conveyed to me,' was his cryptic rejoinder ... and his glance was also very strange....

It was not until she had spent some thought on these words, and the glance, that Juliet realized just what he had meant, and although she was quite alone in the privacy of her cabin she felt the hot colour flood into her cheeks.

Dorian was waiting until she told him that she was expecting a child, and then he would set sail for the island of Thassos....

'He means to keep me prisoner indefinitely,' she breathed. 'For if I'm expecting a child he knows that I can't leave him. What a diabolical mind the man has!'

After she had been fretting and fuming for several hours another aspect of the situation flashed into Juliet's consciousness with the speed of lightning.

'This,' she said, her eyes alive for the first time in weeks, 'is my chance. Oh, Dorian, you're not nearly so clever as you think!'

Over dinner that evening she said, feigning a shyness he had never seen before,

'Dorian ... I've been feeling tired lately, and not too well. You remember that I felt faint one day?'

As she expected the dark eyes flickered—and she thought she detected a hint of satisfaction appear in them as, pretending to blush, she swiftly put her hands up to her cheeks.

'I remember,' softly and inquiringly. 'You seemed to think the heat had affected you.'

She nodded, lowering her eyelashes.

'I d-don't now believe it w-was the heat....' She had

not told a lie—not that she would have felt guilty even if she had, since she considered that all was fair in this war which was being waged between her husband and herself.

'I see.' He nodded his head. 'You're expecting a child, I take it?'

She frowned at his cold accents, at his matter-of-factness over something that should be talked about in gentle, tender tones. However, it was only a part she was acting, so his attitude was of no real importance in circumstances such as these.

'I'm n-not sure, but I think....'

'It's very likely,' he told her in the same matter-of-fact voice. 'Yes, this is what I've been waiting for.' He looked at her across the table. 'We're visiting Rhodes tomorrow; after that we'll sail for home.'

She said, keeping all emotion from her voice,

'Aren't you afraid that, once we get ashore, I'll run out on you?'

Confidently he shook his head, then said the words she expected him to say.

'You'll not tackle this business alone, without the care and financial assistance that I can give you.'

Juliet nodded her head, indicating that she was resigned to staying with him.

'You have me just where you want me,' she murmured.

'Yes. The tables are well and truly turned, aren't they, Juliet?'

Ignoring this, she asked,

'What happens when—er—when the child is born?'

'If you want to go then you're free to do so.'

'I see. And I leave the child behind, I understand?'

For a fleeting moment he seemed unable to frame his words, and he turned his head away from her, as if to hide his expression. When presently he did speak his voice was strangely edged with huskiness.

'The child will be your payment to me for what you've done.' His head was still turned from her, and suddenly she wanted to see his expression, for she was sure his eyes were shadowed. He still cared for her, then? It seemed impossible . . . and yet. . . .

'Do you expect me to leave my child?' she asked, and only then did he turn.

There was no sign of pain in his eyes.

'A woman of your type doesn't want to be hampered with a child,' he said harshly. 'You'll be wanting to hunt around for another wealthy man.'

Flinching at this, Juliet herself turned away. Why did her husband's harshness hurt all at once? Why, when discussing a child like this, did she suddenly want him to be less hostile with her? It was all so utterly absurd, since she was merely fooling him in order to gain her freedom.

She said, rather hesitantly, lest he should become suspicious all at once,

'When we get back to Thassos, Dorian, shall I be free to go about?'

'Free?'

'You know what I mean? Here, I'm a prisoner. Surely I'm not to be locked up at home?'

'As I said, you'll not leave me until after the child is born. You'll be quite free, Juliet.' She said nothing, keeping her exultation carefully hidden. Free. . . . She could run out on him so easily from Thassos. 'In fact,' Dorian was saying, 'you are free from now on. We shall go ashore together when we get to Rhodes.'

'I can leave this boat at last?' A deep sigh escaped her as she added, quite spontaneously and without realizing that she appeared very far removed from the heartless gold-digger which she was supposed to be, 'Oh, Dorian, you have no idea how I shall enjoy that!'

He seemed to give a start, then instantly regained his cool exterior. But he did say, regarding her with the most odd expression,

'There's something very strange about you, Juliet.' He waited, half expecting a response, but she cautiously held her tongue, vitally aware that she could find herself in deep waters. 'Have you nothing to say about that?' he questioned at length, and she merely shook her head and said no, she had nothing at all to say about it. For a while it was a near thing for her and she held her breath, wondering if he would allow the matter to drop. To her inexpressible relief he shrugged his shoulders and changed the subject.

The yacht was moored in the harbour of Mandraki; Juliet gazed from the deck of *Nereus* to the colourful scene of flowers and gardens, imposing buildings and windmills. All along the waterfront were numerous pleasure boats, white and stately, lording it over the little caiques which bobbed about with a sort of gay abandon.

Dorian, coming to stand beside her, asked if she were ready to go ashore.

'Of course.' She was still thrilled by the idea, but now she prudently kept her enthusiasm to herself.

'Come, then, and we'll take a look at Rhodes.'

Island of Roses, she thought . . . and the merest tinge of regret touched her heart. If only this had been a proper honeymoon, spent with someone she loved. . . .

Dismissing this, she said, looking up into his face, 'You've been here before?'

'Yes. I was here about nine years ago.'

And he met Tanya. . . .

'You enjoyed being here?' she just could not help inquiring as they stepped from the boat on to the harbour.

'Very much.' His face became expressionless.

'You were on holiday?'

'I was living here at that time.'

Juliet would have liked to ask more, but his manner forbade it. Nevertheless, she could not help wondering if his thoughts were with her cousin.

'Rhodes....' she murmured and, to herself, 'Where it all began.' If Tanya and her parents had not chosen Rhodes for their holiday then Dorian Coralis and Emily Lowther would never have met ... and he and Juliet Hardy would never have married. What a capricious thing fate was!

Oh, well, it were best to forget her troubles for the time being, she decided as, looking around, she had a vivid impression of a sub-tropical atmosphere, with an unusual clarity of light which is found in Greece alone. Beauty and colour was evident everywhere—in the absorbent crimson of the hibiscus blossoms and the cascades of violet bougainvillaea spreading a riot of glowing colour over the ramparts of the Fortress of the Knights; in the hedges of pink oleander and the flowering trees and shrubs, in the dazzling white arcades reflected in the emerald waters of the harbour. Juliet sighed and, hearing her, Dorian turned, a slight frown appearing on his forehead.

'Why the sigh?' he asked, looking down into her upturned face. 'Don't you want to see some of the island, after all?'

'Certainly I do.'

'You sounded bored.'

'I'd scarcely be bored today—having my freedom like this.'

'Is that sarcasm?' he wanted to know, and it did seem that a glint appeared in his eyes.

'It is not.' A pause and then, 'Dorian, can we hoist a flag of truce—just for the next few hours?'

Silence; she saw his lips compress. However, when eventually he spoke his voice was devoid of hostility as he agreed with her suggestion.

'It will be far more pleasant than walking about in silence—or near silence,' he added. But another long silence did follow, a silence which Juliet several times attempted to break, but found she was enveloped in a net of awkwardness from which she seemed quite unable to disengage herself. And so it was Dorian who eventually brought the silence to an end by saying, 'I suggest we take a look at the Old City first; it's the part of the town that's inside the walls. I think you'll be quite enchanted with it.'

He took her along the famous Street of the Knights, a narrow thoroughfare which still retained its fourteenth-century character—the particular style of architecture used for housing the Knights of St John. Massive coats of arms were carved above the stone porches, and through the wide archways of the ancient houses could be seen fascinating paved courtyards and shady arbours, steps of stone leading to balconies draped with flowers or to roof gardens tantalizingly hidden from view by the façade of the building itself. At one end of the street was the Palace of the Grand Master, and Juliet immediately commented on the fact of its having a distinctly French influence.

'The first six Grand Masters were French,' Dorian informed her. 'So it's not surprising that the style of building is French in character. I believe that the Palace of the Popes in Avignon is very similar to this.' They strolled on, as did many other couples, but these were more often than not walking hand in hand. A curious chill seemed to pass through Juliet's body, the poignant chill of something lost—or was it something out of reach?

'Can we sit down?' she asked, suddenly affected by the heat. 'I'd like a cool drink, Dorian.'

'Of course.' Soon he had her in the shade of a cedar tree, under which was a small table and two chairs. The café was run by a Turk, who came from his shop at once to take their order, also that of another couple who were seated beneath a nearby, thickly-foliaged tree. Other people were seated about, at tables that were spaced out on a pink-stoned pavement bordered by low walls over which tumbled semi-tropical creepers, blazoning the area with scarlet, gold and purple flowers. Soft *bouzouki* music drifted from the direction of the shop. Over at one side of the pavement a group of dusky-faced men lounged in their chairs, playing *tavli*, while others played with well-worn 'worry beads'—*komboli*—a pastime that was said to be good for the nerves.

'Do you feel all right?' Dorian spoke to her, bringing her attention from the group of men. 'You're looking rather pale.' He sounded anxious, she thought, and suddenly a sense of shame and guilt swept over her. Misinformed as he was, he naturally felt some anxiety about her, if only because he wanted the child. And as she looked into his face and saw the tightness of his mouth and the dark concern in his eyes, she could scarcely resist the temptation to be honest with him and so relieve his mind. But of course she refrained, not only because she knew that, in being honest and confessing that she was not expecting a child, she would be throwing away her chance of freedom, and secondly, she would not have *dared* to be honest—knowing her husband's temper and having experienced the savagery which that temper could produce.

'I'm all right,' she told him, leaning back in her chair and beginning to look around again. The mosque and minaret rose to one side of the square; a fountain sparkled in the sunshine. Tourists lounged idly in rattan chairs, or sauntered about, enjoying the cosmopolitan atmosphere, for Rhodes was a place where many different nationalities could be found.

'You're quite sure?' Dorian broke into her quiet mind wanderings and she smiled spontaneously, without realizing she was doing it. Dorian's eyes flickered, but almost immediately his interest was replaced by an expression of concern. 'You're still somewhat pale.'

'I'm quite sure.' Juliet injected a bright note into her voice, and she never did know just why she fobbed him off in this way, since she actually did feel very much under the weather. The sun was affecting her and she felt sick. But she contrived to appear well, and she supposed the reason for this must be that she wanted to prolong the enjoyment she was deriving from this unexpected spell of freedom.

After their refreshments they wandered on, to explore the new part of the town with its parks blazing with exotic colour, its stately buildings lining the shore. The shops were a dream, and Juliet would very much have liked to stop and window-gaze, but Dorian was obviously not in the mood to pander to this kind of whim. She saw him glance into the windows of the jewellers each time one was reached ... and she knew without any doubt at all that, in ordinary circumstances, he would quite literally have showered lovely gifts upon her, gifts she would remember as being bought on their honeymoon. Another sigh escaped her; she felt restless and unanchored, as if she were wandering in a void, quite alone. She was acutely conscious of a strange yearning—but a yearning for what? She was unable to tell.

It was beginning to get dark when Dorian said,

'It's time we went back to the yacht.'

She nodded, acutely aware of a weakness in her legs. The faintness had returned and all she wanted was to rest. They were almost at the harbour when Dorian seemed to sense that something was amiss.

'You're not well,' he asserted, and now she readily owned that she did feel off-colour. 'Why didn't you admit it sooner?' he demanded wrathfully, and once again she was overwhelmed with guilt, for it was an undoubted fact that it was her "condition" that concerned him. She *must* confess, she decided, and take the consequences.

'Dorian—I—I....' She remembered no more, for a blackness came over her; she was in bed when she came to and the nurse who was in the room informed her that she was in the Hotel des Roses.

'You've got a touch of the sun,' she added, smiling and filling a glass with some sort of liquid. 'I'll tell your husband that you've come round.'

'I'm sorry, Dorian,' Juliet was apologizing a few moments later when her husband was standing by the bed, looking down at her. 'It was stupid of me not to have told you sooner how I was feeling.'

'Well, so long as it's nothing more serious,' he returned. 'How are you feeling now?'

'I feel all right.' She paused a moment. 'Dorian, I've a confession to make——'

'Mr Coralis.' The nurse had returned, a look of concern on her face. 'You're wanted at the reception desk. I believe something has happened to your yacht.'

'My——?' He was gone on the instant, returning

about ten minutes later with the news that *Nereus* had been rammed by a large motor cruiser.

'Is she very badly damaged?' asked Juliet in some concern.

'The repairs will take a week at least,' was his grim and wrathful reply. 'Either we can stay here or fly home—I'll make up my mind later. Meanwhile, I've booked us in for tonight.' He looked down at her, having completely forgotten that she had said she had a confession to make. 'I haven't booked a dinner yet. Will you be able to get up, do you think?'

'Yes—oh, yes!' she exclaimed, happy at the idea of taking dinner in the hotel. 'I'm perfectly all right now that I've rested.'

He examined her face, seemed satisfied, and said,

'Very well; I'll order dinner for about half past eight to nine.'

CHAPTER EIGHT

SOFT music and silent-footed waiters, candlelight and flowers; superb food and sparkling wine, crystal glass and silver.... This was the restaurant of the Hotel des Roses, and Juliet and Dorian were dining at a table by a small fountain, fairly secluded, but not as intimately cut off as some of the tables Dorian had chosen during those days of his brief courtship.

'Juliet.' Dorian's soft voice reached her from across the table. 'Your fish is getting cold.'

'I'm sorry.' She had been gazing around, envying the gaiety of the people about her, people who laughed and chatted and danced ... people who were in harmony with one another.

The wine waiter appeared unobtrusively and filled up her glass; at a table in the middle of the restaurant steaks were ablaze over spirit lamps. The whole atmosphere was one of romance, designed to excite both the palate and the senses.

Suddenly—to her own amazement—Juliet wanted to dance with her husband, and she glanced across at him with eyes that invited. But although his eyes, meeting hers, understood her invitation, Dorian merely glanced away again. A feeling of flatness came over Juliet and to her amazement and horror she actually felt a tear seep through from the back of her eye and hang on her lashes. Swiftly requiring a handkerchief, she remembered with some considerable dismay that she had left her evening bag in the bedroom. A quick word of excuse to her husband and she was gone.

On her return she found her way blocked by two

women who, while awaiting attention from a waiter who would show them to their table, were standing just inside the restaurant looking around the room. Both had their backs to Juliet, and with a sort of vague disinterest she found herself mentally contrasting the seductive curves of the younger woman with the plumpness of the other. New arrivals.... This too was an automatic intrusion into a mind that was concerned mainly with getting its owner back to the table where her husband was sitting. A murmured 'Excuse me,' had scarcely left Juliet's lips when two things happened that caused her heart to give a great painful lurch before beginning to thud with mad and sickening speed against her ribs.

The elder woman turned her head, while the younger, sweeping forward into the restaurant, was exclaiming, 'Dorian! But how perfectly marvellous to see you again!'

Many heads turned, and many amused smiles came to the lips of the diners who had heard the exclamation.

Juliet stood stock still, wondering if she looked as white as she felt. The woman had moved to one side, although the disappearance of her daughter from her side had provided ample room for Juliet to pass.

'Mrs Lowther?' A waiter smilingly made the inquiry and the woman nodded her head, having given Juliet a perfunctory glance. 'This way, please....' The words were scarcely heard by Juliet, who moved, with a sort of mechanical pressure, towards the table she had just a few moments ago left. Dorian had risen to his feet; what he said was so quiet that Juliet failed to hear even one word from this distance. Tanya was glowing, using those eyes and lashes with more deftness than ever.

'Imagine meeting in the same place as before!

Dorian, it must be fate!' Juliet was closer now, but neither of the two had yet become aware of her presence. Dorian, at whose face Juliet was looking in profile, wore that inscrutable mask which had become very familiar to her by now, so she had no way of knowing how he was reacting to this meeting with the girl who once had been his pillow friend. Both had been eight years younger then; neither looked too much older now.

'You have company, I see,' from Dorian whose eyes were following the waiter as he took Mrs Lowther to her table.

'Yes! And as you're dining alone, I think we really ought to join you—and drink some special wine to celebrate....' Tanya's voice trailed away to silence as, glancing down at the table, she realized that Dorian was not, in fact, dining alone.

And at this moment he became aware of Juliet's presence.

'Tanya—meet my wife. Juliet, this is Tanya, an old friend of mine.' Urbane the tone; Dorian was carrying off the situation with superb finesse.

Tanya seemed suddenly to go cold, thought Juliet, who noticed the slight tremor that passed through her body.

'Your wife?' Tanya soon recovered and a swift smile leapt to her lips. 'I'm happy to meet you, Juliet.' Her eyes belied the affability of her voice, and the content of her words. For the look she gave Juliet was one that could only be described as baleful. There was envy too, in that glance, for it took in Juliet's lovely features, the glory of her hair. It took in also the expensive dress which Juliet wore, and the diamond necklace and earrings which, with the star in her hair, formed the set which had been Dorian's wedding present to his wife.

'Juliet....' The name was now repeated, slowly. 'An unusual name, even though it belonged to *the* Juliet. I once knew a girl called Juliet,' she added, and her cousin's heart began to thump again. However, the waiter was hovering close by and Tanya was soon being led to her table.

Juliet sat down, watching her husband's face closely. What were his thoughts at this moment? Was he wishing he were free so that he could indulge in an affair with his old flame?

'Madam, you are not drinking your wine.' The good-humoured admonishment came from the lips of the head waiter who, Juliet had noticed, had gone round the room, from table to table, treating the occupants of each as if they were the only people in the room who really mattered. 'Is it not to your liking?'

She managed a smile in response to his.

'It's very good,' she said, and took up her glass.

Her husband looked curiously at her when presently the head waiter left their table to approach the one next to it.

'You haven't evinced much interest in Tanya,' he said, and only then did it occur to Juliet that she should in fact have put a few interested questions to him. But she had refrained for two reasons: she knew all the answers anyway, and, more important, she would have felt deceitful in evincing ignorance of a woman who was her own cousin. However, as it appeared that he was to consider it most odd indeed if she said nothing at all about Tanya, she phrased a question, to which he replied,

'Yes, we did meet here, as she mentioned.'

'She also mentioned the word fate?' Juliet found she was keenly interested in his reply to this.

It was some time before she received it.

'Perhaps she thought I was still single.'

'I see....' Juliet looked down at her plate. 'And if you had been?'

Another silence. The soft strains of *Some Enchanted Evening* drifted sweetly on to the air as if coming through a mist of tulle. Juliet glanced up just in time to catch the glance that her husband cast across the room, and she found herself painfully asking if the tune meant something to Tanya and Dorian. And because of this she turned her head. Tanya was looking directly at Dorian....

'I don't quite understand your question, Juliet.' Dorian spoke at last, and he was faintly brisk now, and his attention had returned to the food upon his plate. Juliet was sitting very still, conscious of Tanya's dark eyes burning into her back.

'She might have thought—thought....' Juliet's voice faltered; she abandoned the question temporarily and asked another. 'It seems that you and she were more than just friends?'

The smile that touched the hard outline of his mouth was as inscrutable as the expression in his eyes.

'I believe you are not obtuse, my dear,' he said.

Delicately the colour tinted her cheeks.

'You and she were ... lovers...?'

Dorian lifted his eyebrows at this direct but hesitantly-spoken question.

'I don't tell tales out of school, Juliet.' Lifting his wineglass, he held it to the candlelight, gently moving it so that the wine caught the glow.

His wife looked at him while his attention was thus employed; she wondered what he would have to say were she to reveal all she knew.

'But you have admitted that you were more than friends,' she insisted. 'At least, I took it as an admission when you said just now that I'm not obtuse.'

'We were very good friends. Shall we put it that way?'

She nodded, but automatically.

'So in that case she might have thought she and you could begin again, and perhaps—perhaps come together permanently?' The first question was out now and she looked directly at him as she awaited his response.

'Permanently?' Dorian lifted his straight black brows and added, 'What exactly do you mean by that?'

'Marriage...?' Why, she asked herself, did she feel a hint of pain in the region of her heart?

'I'm married,' came the soft reply. 'And likely to stay that way.'

'But if you and I should have a divorce——'

'In Greece we don't regard divorce in the same light as you in the west.'

'So, whatever happens, you're expecting me to remain your wife?'

Silence. She sensed a sudden anger rising within him.

'We'll change the subject,' he told her harshly.

'It was your idea to talk about your friend,' she reminded him.

'Come,' he snapped, ignoring this, 'we'll dance!'

From the moment she slipped into his arms Juliet sensed the keen eyes of Tanya upon her. Her mother, too, was watching just as interestedly and when on reaching their table Dorian stopped to speak to her, and to introduce his wife, Mrs Lowther's gaze was concentrated and examining. Juliet met her eyes unflinchingly, confident that she would never be recognized. The face of the woman who had caused her such misery as a child had even harsher lines now, and her mouth had hardened even more with the years. It was now a thin line above a chin that had doubled, protruding over a scraggy neck. Her hair was white and thin; her scalp shone pinkly through it. With an involuntary shudder Juliet twisted her body, bringing herself round, for the very sight of the woman nauseated her.

'Is something wrong?' Dorian asked a moment later when they had moved away from the table. She had failed to change her expression quickly enough and he frowned in puzzlement. 'You look as though your mind's occupied by something exceedingly distasteful.'

At this she almost smiled, but knowing her husband so well, she cautiously refrained. Questions just now could become far too awkward for her to answer ... in which case, Dorian would instantly become suspicious....

Not that he could possibly make a guess at the truth. No; and she did not suppose he would believe anyone who told him that he had married Emily Lowther—should anyone ever be in a position to do so, that was.

'As a matter of fact,' she said when it seemed that Dorian would insist on some comment from her, 'I was thinking of something distasteful, but it isn't important.' And before he had time to probe, had he wished to do so, she went on to chat, about the decor and the lighting, the excellent food and the haunting music.

Dorian remained silent, listening to her. She sensed a faint puzzlement in his manner, and on looking up she saw that a thoughtful expression had settled on his face.

It was much later, when Dorian and Juliet had been for a stroll and were re-entering the hotel, that they came face to face with Tanya once more. She had been sitting in the lounge, drinking a brandy and soda and smoking a cigarette, but seeing them enter she rose and without any sort of preliminary asked them to join her. Dorian looked at his wife and it was plain that, on this occasion at least, the decision was hers. She hesitated, but the temptation to be in Tanya's company was too great. It would be a most diverting situation, she decided, amusement already revealed in her eyes.

'That would be nice,' she said quietly, so she and Dorian followed Tanya as she went back to her table in the lounge. Flopping into a deep wide armchair, Tanya flung out a hand, indicating the other two seats. Juliet and Dorian took possession of them and he ordered drinks from the waiter who instantly appeared.

'Are you on holiday?' was the first thing which Tanya asked.

'Sort of,' from Dorian as he cast a swift glance at his wife.

'Sort of?'

'We're on our honeymoon,' submitted Juliet, some little devil of revenge getting into her. 'We're sailing to the islands aboard Dorian's yacht——'

'Yacht?' Tanya's tone was like chipped ice. 'You didn't own a yacht when I knew you, Dorian.' She was not looking at him, but at Juliet, a most odd expression in her eyes. It was the same sort of expression she had seen in the eyes of Mr Godfrey on the occasion of her return to West Havington. Juliet had wondered if he were puzzled by her voice, feeling he had once known someone whose voice was similar in tone. Now she had the same idea about Tanya, sure that she was trying to place the voice. Perhaps Tanya would eventually realize the connection, but that was as far as she would get, since not by any stretch of imagination could she carry the similarity any further. Most certainly she would never conceive the idea that Juliet Coralis and the drab little slave, Emily Lowther, were one and the same.

'I acquired it only about a year ago,' Dorian was saying, and he too was looking at Juliet. Plainly her talk of a honeymoon had surprised him ... especially as she was talking to a total stranger—or so he believed.

'I'd love to see it. May I?'

'Of course.' The answer came at once and it did seem to Juliet that he showed more than a little eagerness to have his old flame aboard his yacht.

'Fine!' Tanya favoured him with a dazzling smile, and as far as she was concerned, Dorian's lovely young bride might not have been there at all. 'When, Dorian?' she asked, leaning towards him so that her bare arm was in contact with the sleeve of his jacket. 'Tomorrow?'

Dorian shook his head, saying that as the yacht was damaged, it would be better to wait until Saturday, which was three days hence.

'If that doesn't suit you,' he added, 'then you yourself can make the date. You're here for two weeks, you said?'

'That's right. Yes, Saturday will do fine.'

'It's settled, then.' Dorian seemed to be deliberately avoiding his wife's eyes, an action that infuriated her. Also, both he and Tanya had ignored her when making the arrangements, and now Tanya was actually smirking!—with satisfaction at the way Dorian had left his wife out of the discussion. Although she tried her best to keep a rein on her temper Juliet found herself saying sharply,

'Am I not to be consulted about this?'

Both her companions stared at her, and she found herself colouring. She was so filled with anger that she could have got up and stalked away, but she thought twice about such an action, for she was not going to leave these two alone.

'I'm sorry,' said Dorian, surprising her. 'I took it for granted that this arrangement would suit you.'

Juliet bit her lip, aware that she had come out of this in a very bad light.

The drinks arrived and as Juliet's spurt of anger had died by this time, the conversation progressed on friendly lines. Tanya and Dorian were talking of experiences and various aspects of their lives since last they had met, and as she listened Juliet waited all the while for Tanya to mention her marriage and its breakdown, but the girl's confidences fell short of this. Nor did she mention her father's losses, and the great fall in the value of his estate. In fact, decided Juliet, Tanya was not saying very much at all. And, strangely, neither was Dorian. Within her Juliet knew a profound feeling of restlessness and anxiety. For it would seem that these two would much rather have been on their own ... so that confidences could have gone much deeper.

During the conversation Juliet learned that her aunt had been ill, and the doctor had advised a change of scene and climate. So, said Tanya, they decided to take a holiday in Rhodes, since they had enjoyed themselves so much on that other occasion.

'What a coincidence,' she went on, 'meeting you here again like this.' She was leaning towards Dorian and again his wife might not have been there for all the notice she took of her. However, Dorian soon brought her into the conversation, but as soon as she spoke she saw Tanya's eyes flicker, and a thin line of concentration appear along her forehead. It was as if she were striving to recapture something as elusive as a dream. Amused, Juliet found all at once that she was really enjoying herself, disguised in this way, and being so confident of the impenetrability of that disguise. And so she began to ask questions, delighting in the answers she received.

'How long is it since you and Dorian met here, Tanya—I can call you Tanya, can't I?'

'But of course!' Tanya was gushing suddenly. 'How long...? It was over nine years ago; I was here on holiday with my mother and father.'

'So you haven't seen each other for nine years?'

'Dorian came over to England about a year later—well——' she looked at Dorian. 'It was a little less than a year, wasn't it?'

No answer; Dorian's whole attention was with his wife and she knew he was somewhat nonplussed that she should be talking in this way to a woman who, he had freely admitted, was at one time more than a friend.

'Tanya's asked you a question, Dorian.' Juliet would have very much liked to insert the word darling, but she feared that her husband's surprise would be such that he might just give a visible start. But undoubtedly the situation was diverting, even without the endearments, since Juliet could without much difficulty sense her cousin's jealousy.

How satisfying it would be to tell Tanya who she was!

'Umm? What did you say, Tanya?'

'It wasn't important. Juliet was wanting to know how long it is since we last met.' She paused, but he did not vouchsafe the information asked for.

'You stayed with Tanya's parents?'

He nodded and frowned.

'Yes.'

Juliet turned to Tanya.

'Whereabouts do you live?'

'West Havington. Do you know it?'

'I've certainly heard of it.'

'Where was your home?'

Juliet told her, mentioning only the town where she had lived with Mr and Mrs Manley. Like Dorian, Tanya assumed that Juliet had lived with her parents. To Juliet's relief she probed no further regarding these 'parents' but did go on to ask how Juliet came to know West Havington.

'My friend and I went for a run in the car one day,' answered Juliet imperturbably. 'We came upon this village—it was becoming built up, of course, but I could imagine it being a rather pretty place at one time.'

'It's built up?' from Dorian in some surprise. 'That's rather a pity. What about your place? Has it been affected?'

Tanya nodded her head.

'Unfortunately, yes. We've a new estate which has come right up to the borders of our land. It's blocked our view altogether.'

'Your father will be upset about that.'

'He's had a breakdown over it.'

'I'm sorry.' Dorian sounded sincere, but yet Juliet had the impression that he was not too interested in the misfortunes of the Lowthers. This impression brought back an idea she had a long time ago, when Dorian was the Lowthers' guest. He had seemed faintly contemptuous of them. 'Why doesn't he sell out and find somewhere more secluded?'

A small hesitation from Tanya and then,

'The house has lost its value, Dorian. No one wants it any more.' She paused and frowned. 'In those days when you were our guest our kind of house was at a premium. Everybody wanted that type of place—secluded, with magnificent views....' She shrugged her shoulders and lapsed into silence.

Juliet said quietly,

'You live with your parents, then?'

Tanya nodded, but she looked away as she spoke.

'Yes; I live with them at the Grange.'

'You—never married?' It was Dorian who spoke, and Juliet noticed that he was watching her cousin closely.

'I did, yes, Dorian....' Tanya looked into his eyes ... and her own shadowed. To Juliet it seemed that her cousin was trying to send him a silent message. 'It was a mistake ... I ought to have known it would be....' The look was fixed; Dorian's face was devoid of expression and so his wife had no means of learning just how he was taking this.

'You're divorced?' he inquired, and Tanya had said yes, she had been divorced for some years. 'Never mind, you'll probably have better luck next time.'

'There won't be a next time, Dorian.' Tanya's glance shifted to Juliet, and that baleful light once again entered her eyes. 'I feel that the mistake was made a long time ago ... before I met George and married him.'

Juliet could have gasped. What blatant outspokenness! She was actually telling Dorian that *he* should have married her.

'Have you no brothers and sisters?' from Juliet who, although aware of her hypocrisy, was, nevertheless, enjoying herself immensely. 'There are only the three of you?'

'Yes—now, there are.'

'Now? Emily left, then?' Dorian spoke without much interest, little knowing just how his words were affecting his wife. 'She didn't manage to find herself a husband, surely?' At this addition Juliet experienced a deep and burning conflict of emotions, her anger battling with an almost irrepressible desire to laugh.

'Not that I know of,' contemptuously from Tanya. 'She ran off soon after your visit——'

'Ran off?—with some man, you mean?'

'It probably was with a man. Mother and Father certainly believed so. We've never heard one word from her since. This after all we did for her. As you know, she'd have been in an institution if we hadn't taken her in.'

'That's ingratitude for you!' Dorian flicked a hand to call the waiter. 'What are you drinking, Juliet—Tanya?' They told him and he ordered. When the waiter had gone Juliet said, a little devil well and truly established within her by this time,

'This—Emily was adopted by your parents?'

'She was my cousin; her parents were killed when she was six, and we took her in, gave her a lovely home, pretty clothes, and food. She gave us nothing in return, did she, Dorian?'

'Only a lot of trouble,' he answered grimly. But he stopped there and Juliet did wonder if he were thinking that he himself had never seen Emily dressed in pretty clothes.

'She certainly sounds most ungrateful,' murmured Juliet, but then she added, 'You're sure she wasn't lonely, feeling sort of pushed out?'

'Certainly not. We gave her everything, including love!'

Love.... How could Tanya sit there and lie like this, without so much as a blush or even a flicker of an eyelid?

'And you've never heard of her since? Didn't you try to find her at all?'

'We inquired at the police station in the nearest town, but they never found her.'

'It savours of a mystery,' said Juliet. 'I mean—she might have been murdered, or killed in an accident.'

Tanya merely shrugged at this.

'It would probably have been a good thing if she had. You see, she was no good—morally, that was.'

At this Juliet actually gave a gasp. A girl like Tanya, to denounce anyone else as morally no good! Anger won now, over Juliet's amusement, and she was aware of the swift rise of colour that fused her cheeks.

'I cannot help feeling that you ought to have done something about finding her,' said Juliet tautly. 'If your parents accepted responsibility for her then surely they felt it incumbent on them to make exhaustive inquiries when she was missing?' Both Tanya and Dorian were staring strangely at her, but Juliet for the moment cared not one jot that they might be surprised and puzzled by her words. 'How old was this girl?' she added, looking straight at Tanya.

'Seventeen—or almost so.'

'Poor thing! She was very young to be going out into the world all on her own.'

'We think she went with a man....' Tanya spoke slowly, her eyes narrowed slightly. 'You seem very interested in my cousin Emily,' she added curiously, and Juliet began to wonder if she should hold her tongue from now on. But she could not, and she said that she supposed she felt a little sorry for the girl.

'It can't be pleasant—knowing one is totally dependent upon the charity of others,' she added, refusing to meet her husband's eyes which, she sensed, were still regarding her with a most odd expression. 'But I suppose you and your parents were kind enough to refrain from reminding her of her position?'

A deep frown gathered on Tanya's forehead. She said slowly, and very softly,

'When you visited West Havington that time, did anyone talk to you?'

'Talk?' repeated Juliet with well-feigned surprise. 'Why should they?' Her confidence, gained during her schooling and from the wonderful influence of her benefactors, Mr and Mrs Manley, was well to the fore at this time and she was more than a match for the girl who, for years, had made her feel like something that had crawled out of the earth. 'I don't think I understand you?'

Dorian came in then, aware that there might be antagonism in the air if he allowed the two girls to continue without his interruption.

'Does all this matter?' he asked, forcing a laugh. 'Juliet, my dear, none of this really concerns you——'

'I couldn't help feeling that Juliet met someone in the village who was ready to gossip about us—and Emily,' broke in Tanya rudely. 'You know how they gossiped when you arrived, Dorian; it was a nine days' wonder. And so it's feasible that someone talked to Juliet, for, amazing though it seems, there are still one or two who sympathized with the wretched girl, believing that we treated her badly—this in spite of the fact that she almost brought disgrace upon us.'

'Disgrace?' inserted Juliet in a very soft tone. 'What sort of disgrace?'

Tanya laughed and said,

'Your husband will tell you some time, if you ask him nicely.'

Burning with anger, Juliet could never afterwards understand how she managed to remain so calm.

'Dorian,' she said, 'tell me now.'

He glowered at her and snapped,

'We'll change the subject, if you don't mind!'

Another laugh rang out as Tanya looked maliciously at Juliet. She said amusedly,

'And now we've got you guessing, haven't we?' Juliet gave her a look of contempt and she coloured. 'You still haven't answered my question,' she said, clearly trying to hide the fact that she was put out of countenance. 'Did anyone talk to you about Emily? I ask simply because of your interest in the girl.'

Becoming really alert now, Juliet was swift to realize that she really had gone just that little bit too far. She decided not to go any farther and, resorting to that superior manner which she had adopted before, she raised her eyebrows and said,

'I am not in the habit of gossiping with strangers.'

Her cousin reddened again, but now her eyes were on Juliet's hair, for having swung her head in an unconscious gesture, Juliet had brought her lovely hair into the rays of the lamp on the wall above her; they highlighted the pure gold, and brought out the copper glints. This was the beautiful hair which Juliet had once darkened in the hope that, as a brunette, she would attract the notice of the man with whose picture she had fallen in love.

CHAPTER NINE

Juliet sat on the lawn with a book on her lap—an unopened book, for her eyes were on the couple playing tennis a few yards away: Tanya, exquisitely feminine in very brief white shorts, and Dorian, his dark skin contrasting vividly with the white shirt and shorts that he wore. The laughter of the two would ring out now and then, and on one occasion when this occurred Juliet heard a passing couple discussing the pair on the tennis court.

'Aren't they a well-matched pair? Are they husband and wife, do you think?'

'Probably....'

The couple strolled on and Juliet heard no more. But she was burning with fury ... and she was in a fighting mood! And so it was somewhat unfortunate that Mrs Lowther chose this time to come and join her, bringing a deck-chair from some distance and placing it on the grass beside Juliet.

'My daughter seems to be enjoying herself,' was the woman's first comment, which naturally served to increase Juliet's anger. 'Dorian, too——'

'So I see, Mrs Lowther. I'm not blind!'

Her aunt turned to her, and regarded her with that mild but censorious stare which Emily Lowther had known so well, and under which she had so often cringed.

'You're not happy, dear. It's understandable, but you know, you'll have to learn not to be jealous. After all, Dorian's old friends are important to him and you can't expect him to drop them simply because he's married you.'

Juliet gasped, and the colour flooded into her cheeks.

'I am not in need of advice,' she told her aunt acidly. And she opened her book. 'I was intending to read——'

'Now I've made you angrier than you were before——'

'I wasn't angry!'

'Oh, but you were, my dear. It was written all over your face—*and* the fact that you were seething with jealousy. No, please don't interrupt me, Mrs Coralis! What I've got to say will hurt, but it must be said. Dorian and Tanya were once very much in love, and it was a tragedy that they never married. We all expected them to announce their engagement but, for some stupid reason, they decided to part. They've both regretted it——'

'Mrs Lowther,' quivered Juliet, every nerve affected by her anger, 'you appear to forget that you're talking to Dorian's wife!'

'I haven't forgotten....' An almost pained expression settled on her face. 'No, indeed I haven't. But just look at them now—so happy together.' A deep regretful sigh escaped her before she added, 'They've been in each other's company almost continuously for the past day and a half—ever since we arrived, in fact.' She looked darkly at the niece she failed to recognize. 'Can't you see, Mrs Coralis, that they're still in love?'

Again Juliet gasped. The woman must have lost her senses to talk like this—and yet, reflected Juliet, she had always been outspoken to the very point of rudeness. It was her arrogant nature, her attitude of superiority.

'I can only conclude,' said Juliet, assuming an air of great dignity, 'that you are speaking without prior thought. You are rude and unrestrained; your manners are disgraceful—' She picked up her book which had dropped to the grass beside her chair. 'And now, if you will be good enough to leave me, I'll——'

'Manners!' interrupted her aunt. 'You dare to criticize *my* manners? My girl—what about yours!'

So very reminiscent of the aunt she had feared! The tone, the expression, the compression of that ruthless mouth. And suddenly, for no valid or logical reason at all, Juliet was sorry for her aunt. Sorry because she had missed so much in life—being unable to give love, or affection even; being unable to extend compassion where compassion was required, being so totally wrapped in her armour of cold arrogance that no one could get anywhere near her. And now—the disappointment of seeing Dorian Coralis married to someone else, when it had been her profound desire that he should marry her daughter. Something within Juliet thawed, and her fury died. Her voice was edged with kindness when presently she spoke.

'Mrs Lowther, if you want to stay, do so by all means. But let's change the subject.'

For a moment it seemed that her aunt would fail to respond, for her eyes were dark with bitterness and regret as they stared unblinkingly at her lovely daughter who, laughing as she chased after a ball, looked the picture of health and vitality. But at length Mrs Lowther turned her head, and a smile was forced to her lips.

'Yes, of course we'll change the subject. Er—tell me about Dorian's yacht?'

It was a superficial question, put simply because the woman could think of nothing else at the moment.

Juliet obligingly talked, and as she did she suddenly noticed the widening of her aunt's eyes.

'I have it!' she exclaimed. 'Tanya said there was

something about you that seemed familiar—and now I have it!'

'You have?' Juliet's voice faltered and her heart caught. But her composure soon returned and she waited politely for her aunt to continue.

'Yes, it's your voice! It's very similar to that of my niece.'

'Emily—the one who ran away?'

'How do you know that?'

'Tanya talked about her that first evening—when we were in the lounge. You'd gone to bed immediately after dinner, I believe?'

'Ah, yes.' A small pause. 'Tanya didn't mention to me that she'd been talking about Emily. What did she say about her?'

'Not very much,' replied Juliet, lowering her eyelashes. 'I gathered that you weren't very concerned when she ran away from home.'

The woman frowned, but it was not Juliet's words that occupied her thoughts, as her next words betrayed.

'The same voice ... and the same name....'

'Name?' repeated Juliet, unconcerned.

'Emily's other name was Juliet.'

'A strange coincidence,' murmured Juliet. 'Just imagine that!'

Mrs Lowther's frown deepened. She stared at Juliet's hair, then at her face, then her eyes moved to her hands—beautiful hands with long tapering fingers and beautifully shaped nails.

Juliet chuckled inwardly, aware that her aunt was very puzzled indeed. However, if there was anything ready on the woman's lips it was not voiced, for at that moment Dorian and Tanya came over to them, both rather hot and breathless.

'Oh, but it was a marvellous game!' Tanya sat

down on the grass and hugged her knees. 'Phew, but it's warm!'

Mrs Lowther was smiling benignly at Dorian, who was standing close to Tanya, looking down into her animated face.

'Why not take her inside, for a cool drink?' Mrs Lowther suggested, and Juliet froze. What was her aunt trying to do?'

'It's time we were getting cleaned up for lunch,' said Juliet, rising to her feet. 'Are you coming, Dorian?'

His eyes glinted; he said, in a very soft tone,

'Not yet, Juliet.'

She coloured with anger, swallowed the words that rose to her lips and, turning, walked briskly away towards the open french window of the hotel lounge. Having passed into the room she remembered her book, which she had left on the grass and, stepping through the window again, she walked back to the lawn. Several large trees formed a clump close to where Dorian and the two women were, still chatting. Juliet had not meant to approach them unnoticed; it was pure chance that she happened to be behind one huge tree when she heard the words which brought her to an abrupt halt.

'Tanya, I've discovered what it is about Juliet that made you think you'd known her before.'

'Have you, Mother? What is it?'

'Her voice.'

'Voice?' in some puzzlement.

'It has a tone like that of Emily——'

'So it has! Yes—a sort of metallic tone.'

Juliet stiffened. Many people had said that her voice was musical.

'Dorian, surely you noticed the similarity?' Mrs Lowther was saying suddenly, as if the thought had just occurred to her.

'No, I haven't.'

'Dorian wouldn't have, Mother. He never bothered much with Emily, if you remember.'

No—because Emily was invariably in the kitchen, preparing food or washing the dishes, or the clothes—or scrubbing the tiled floor. Juliet was grimly recalling this as Mrs Lowther was speaking again, mentioning the fact that Emily's other name was Juliet.

'Isn't it a most strange coincidence?' she added, and a small silence followed.

'I never knew about Emily's other name,' said Dorian.

'You wouldn't,' returned Tanya. 'We always called her Emily. Mother thought it suited her better than Juliet.'

'*You* thought it suited her better?' Dorian was speaking to Mrs Lowther and, listening, Juliet began to be puzzled by the fact that he was interested enough to proceed with the subject. 'You mean—Emily didn't choose to be called Emily?'

'She always wanted Juliet, but you must admit that a pretty name like that was totally unsuitable for a plain Jane like my niece?'

The colour having flooded into her cheeks, Juliet decided it was best to retreat ... before she said something she would bitterly regret! And so she left her book where it was and went back the way she had come. About a quarter of an hour later her husband entered the bedroom where she was changing, after having had a wash at the basin in the adjoining bathroom. She was in brief undies and immediately picked up a housecoat and put it on. Dorian's eyes glimmered with sardonic amusement, and as this was like fuel to a fire she turned on him, her eyes blazing.

'People are concluding that Tanya's your wife, and

not me! Must you spend so much time with her?'

His dark eyes flickered over her contemptuously.

'What right have you to complain?' he asked harshly. 'Any rights you might have had were forfeited the moment you told me you married me for my money.' His eyes settled on her face; she noticed the depth of brooding in them ... and the merest hint of suspicion. She recalled that he had said that there was something strange about her; he had said it in a way that caused her to wonder if he had some small doubts about the truth of her words when she had told him she had married him for his money.

'Tanya's laughing at me——'

'That'll be a chastening experience for you,' he cut in, his voice like a rasp.

'I'm not having it! I won't be made a laughing-stock!' She was crimson with anger, and she had stamped her foot, an involuntary action which she instantly regretted. 'You're not going to neglect me like this!'

His eyes widened.

'Say that again,' he invited softly—and she did. But it was to her cost. With two great strides he was before her, grasping her arms in a cruel grip that caused her to cry out. 'No woman gives me orders! Get that!'

White to the lips, she tried to get away, but his hold merely tightened until the tears came to her eyes.

'Dorian, you're hurting me——'

'And I'll hurt you more.' He shook her slightly. 'Keep your place, Juliet, or by God you'll regret it!' He released her and she stepped back until she felt the bed against her legs.

'You're going to carry on like this for the whole of our stay?' she managed to inquire at length.

'What do you mean, carry on like this?'

'You know what I mean. Are you going to play

around with Tanya all the time—and leave me on my own?'

'I mean to enjoy myself with Tanya, yes.' Arrogantly he looked down at her, his lips drawn back to show a row of even white teeth. 'I'm sorry if you object, but you've only yourself to blame.'

'So it's revenge?' Secretly she was admitting that she could not really blame him for what he was doing.

'Call it that if you like.' He was unbuttoning his tennis shirt as he went towards the bathroom door. 'In any case, I don't know why you should care; you're intending to leave me in less than a year.'

Leave.... She turned away to the dressing-table, and gazed at her reflection through the mirror. Her plan had been to leave him as soon as she was able—as soon as she got back to Thassos, from where she could escape. But now she was seeing her escape as a clearway for Tanya....

'Supposing I decide not to leave you?' She actually started at her own words, scarcely knowing from where they had come. There was no question of her staying with him; Tanya could have him!

'Then you'll stay.' He spoke over his shoulder before disappearing through the doorway. 'But you'll stay under the conditions which I shall lay down.'

Juliet said, turning her head,

'And what might those be?'

'That you accept the position of a Greek wife——'

'Become a vassal?' she shot at him. 'Never!' She was glaring into the aperture. Dorian made no comment on what she had said; he merely closed the bathroom door.

Tanya moved about the yacht as if she owned it, commenting, touching, praising and appreciating.

'It's glorious! Oh, Dorian, how I'd love to sail on her!'

He glanced at his wife, then said,

'So you shall, Tanya. How about coming back with us to Thassos? You don't have to go home next week, do you?'

'Mother must go ... but I can stay as long as I like.'

'Stay by all means, dear,' said her mother, who had been exploring the sleeping cabin. 'It would be a shame not to take advantage of Dorian's offer.'

Juliet, her face colouring rapidly, stood there, suffering humiliation yet again from the man who had caused her so much humiliation before. He was slaying her with his callousness, punishing her in the only way his pagan heart could devise.

It would not be for long, she assured herself; she would leave him just as soon as they arrived back at the villa.

'Must we go back?' Tanya was saying when at last Dorian said that it was time they were returning to the hotel. 'I could stay aboard, now that I'm here.'

'That, I'm afraid, is impossible. You must remember that she is undergoing repair.'

'Of course, dear Dorian; I do understand.' Tanya shone up at him, apparently oblivious of the two other people on board—or of Elias who, watching with some considerable amusement, winked at his friend and actually thumbed in Juliet's direction.

She turned away, half inclined to desert Dorian immediately she got back to the hotel, for it would be the simplest thing to get a plane to take her back to England. However, she saw no reason why she should leave all her possessions behind. And in any case, almost all her money was at the villa, being left there at the request of Dorian who had told her that she would not be needing money as he himself would supply all her wants.

During the next three days Tanya and Dorian were never apart for very long, while Juliet, left alone, decided that, as long as she was on the island of Rhodes, she might as well do some sightseeing. That the whole situation was ludicrous could not be denied, for there was Dorian, taking an old flame about with him, while his very new bride went off on the coach trips organized by the hotel staff.

'Where are you going today?' Dorian asked one morning when he and Juliet were at the breakfast table.

'What do you care?' she snapped.

He seemed faintly amused at this flare of temper.

'I don't,' was his cool rejoinder. 'I was merely being polite.'

'Thanks. Don't trouble!'

'Juliet,' he said softly, 'be very careful.'

She looked at him, her face pale but coldly dispassionate.

'You said we'd drop the hostility while we were here,' she reminded him.

'I did,' he agreed, but went on to add, 'However, I didn't know then that Tanya was going to be here.'

She swallowed hard, bewildered by the fact that she was feeling hurt by his neglect of her. And was she experiencing something else as well? Jealousy...? No, it could not be!

'It's disgraceful of you to invite Tanya to come aboard the yacht, and sail with us to Thassos.'

'Tanya happens to be a friend of mine.'

Suddenly Juliet laughed, a laugh devoid of mirth.

'You must be the first man ever to take his pillow-friend on his honeymoon!' She laughed again, almost in his face; his eyes narrowed smoulderingly as they met hers across the width of the breakfast table.

'Just what makes you assume she's my—er—pillow-friend?'

'She was once, so it's feasible for me to conclude that she's fallen into the same role again.'

'She was once?' he repeated. 'I've never said so.'

'I know she was——' Juliet stopped, almost clapping a dismayed hand to her mouth. Dorian was looking at her with a wide and questioning stare, as well he might.

'You ... know she was...?' He continued to stare, noting Juliet's fluctuating colour, and the fact that she was swallowing hard, obviously put out by her own slip. 'What a strange thing to say, Juliet.'

She looked down at her hands, which were both in her lap.

'I can tell,' she floundered, still avoiding his penetrating gaze. 'It's—it's obvious.'

'Oh, why is it obvious?'

Juliet gestured impatiently.

'It just is, that's all.'

'I'm afraid you'll have to explain more fully than that,' he said in a very soft tone. 'You've made an assertion and therefore you'll provide me with some reason for that assertion.'

Frowningly she shook her head. Having successfully made an effort to regain her composure, she was now more able to look at him in the eye and say,

'I'm not willing to give you my reason, Dorian. It's enough that I'm convinced that you and Tanya were lovers once.'

Silence, long and profound. At length Dorian picked up his knife and began buttering the piece of toast that had lain on his plate for the past few moments.

'I've already said that there's something about you

that I don't understand,' he said. 'Something strange, Juliet.' His dark eyes were again penetrating. 'Yes, very strange indeed.' Thoughtfully he frowned. 'I've already said, also, that you are keeping something back.' He stopped then, but Juliet was disturbed. And feeling she should evince some curiosity, just for appearances' sake, she assumed an expression of incomprehension and asked him what he meant. She was totally unprepared for his response.

'Why did you marry me, Juliet?' Soft the tone, but she actually gave a start, her knife clattering against her plate. Dorian's glance moved to it, then returned to her face.

'You know why,' she hedged, and added just for effect, 'What an unnecessary question to ask!'

'Is it?' with a narrowing of his gaze. 'Tell me, all the same.' Commanding the accents, intense the scrutiny to which he was subjecting her. She felt her heart lurch even though she was reassuring herself about her 'disguise'. 'If you don't tell me the truth, Juliet,' he continued presently, 'I'm quite likely to use my own method of extracting it from you ... and that method could be exceedingly painful for you.'

She paled, acutely aware of the wild thudding of her heart. However, she faced him bravely, and told him that, no matter what his doubts might be, she had married him for his money.

His mouth compressed, denoting anger and impatience, but it was the frown between his eyes that arrested her attention, since it quite clearly showed a deep frustrating puzzlement.

'And yet you're willing to terminate the marriage?' he said at last.

'When I married you I didn't expect you to treat me the way you have.' It was an attempt to justify her decision, but she was under no illusions about its weakness. As far as Dorian was concerned there was no justification that he could see—but then he was totally ignorant of her *real* reason for marrying him.

His dark eyes raked her with contempt; he said icily,

'We don't get very far, do we?'

She looked at him, and without warning she found herself remembering all the hurt she had suffered because of his action, found herself re-living all the humiliation; the scourge of her aunt's tongue came back, causing her to squirm. She recalled how she had cringed under her cousin's amused contempt, how she had wept bitterly at her uncle's denouncement that she was a wanton who had offered herself to his guest. She was remembering those villagers who had been her friends, making life a little more bearable for her by their smiles and greetings and their invitations to her to enter their cottages and share a cup of tea or coffee. All this had come to an end following the scandal which her aunt and cousin had so maliciously spread about her. With her hatred for him taking precedence over all other emotions, she looked arrogantly into his dark face and said,

'I wasn't aware that either of us had the least desire to get very far, as you put it. You don't want me any more than I want you——'

'But yet you object to my inviting Tanya to my home?' he cut in harshly, 'acting as if you're the persecuted wife!' She could not answer, having no patience with the conversation, and so the rest of the meal was eaten in total silence.

Later, she boarded the coach which drew up at the front entrance of the hotel; it took her, along with many other guests, to the village of Lindos, the most famous of the three ancient cities of Rhodes. On the way she looked from the window of the coach, but the passing scene was only vaguely imprinted on her mind ... for persistently intruding was the picture of Dorian and Tanya ... together all the time. Mrs Lowther was delighted at the turn of events, her attitude towards Juliet being one of indifference not unmingled with contempt.

'See those goatskin leggings the women are wearing?' The voice came from her left-hand side and she turned her head. The young man who occupied it was not a guest at the Hotel des Roses and therefore she had not spoken to him when, at the start of the journey, he had come and taken the vacant seat beside her. 'They're worn as a protection against snakes.'

'They are?' she returned politely, swiftly taking in the sun-tanned skin, the open, ready smile, the frank and friendly expression in his hazel eyes.

'Yes.' He paused a moment, staring through the window at her side of the coach. 'Here in Greece,' he continued presently, 'the women are just slaves, while their menfolk are treated like kings.'

'It's a very antiquated idea,' from the seat behind. 'I have lived in Greece, and the way the men treat their wives sickens me.'

Both Juliet and the young man turned their heads. The speaker was a man of about sixty-five and they were soon to learn that he was a writer of travel articles, having taken up writing as a hobby after retiring from business. The three fell into conversation, and when at length the coach reached its destination they all automatically kept together. The older man, Leonard Peverill, was most interesting to chat with; the younger man, Jack Quales, was less knowledgeable about the world in general, but good company for all that.

'Shall we all go up to the Acropolis together?' he suggested as they strolled about the crowded plaza taking a perfunctory look at the tourist shops where, in many of the doorways, women stood and begged them to buy hand-knitted sweaters, or hand-embroidered cloths and blouses. 'There's where we hire the donkeys—over there.'

Juliet smiled; it was impossible to miss the place where the donkeys could be hired; one's nose would guide one there!

A whole caravan of tourists began to snake their way—astride the donkeys—up the narrow stony path towards the Acropolis which, silhouetted against a brilliant blue sky, was a high bluff against the edge of the sea. The buildings on it shone in the sunlight, mellow and awe-inspiring, both the Temple of Athena and the Propylaea having been modelled on their counterparts in Athens. Juliet and her two companions, having handed the donkeys over to a man waiting at the top of the path, mounted the stairway and were soon gazing appreciatively at the small but beautiful Byzantine church.

'If only these numerous guides would stop trying to outshout one another,' complained the older man with a frown. 'I wonder just how many languages are being used here at this moment?' He and the other two were already on Christian name terms, having exchanged names while still on the coach. 'I can hear German and French and ...' he paused a moment, 'Danish and Swedish.'

The place was thronged with visitors; Jack asserted that it was like Piccadilly Circus, then lifted his camera to join the ranks of a couple of hundred others doing the same thing. Leonard asked apologetically if they would mind his strolling off, as he wanted to get down to some note-taking for the article he was intending to write about the ancient buildings of Lindos.

'Not at all,' returned Jack, with rather more eagerness than seemed polite. But, glancing at him, Juliet realized that he was welcoming the prospect of having her company to himself for a while. 'Shall we go over to the castle?' he added, smiling at her. She nodded, glad of his company, and amusedly wondering what he would say were she to inform him that she was here on her honeymoon.

'Let's sit down for a while,' she was saying later, 'I wonder if we can find somewhere a little more quiet.'

'I admit it's like a market-place just here. I know—how about returning to the town and finding a quiet little *taverna* where we can sit under the shade of the vines and drink iced orange juice?'

'That would be nice, but what about Leonard?'

'If we can locate him we can tell him to join us when he's ready. He'll have to find us, but that shouldn't be difficult as we'll be sitting outside the *taverna,* not inside.' He glanced around. 'There he is! I'll run over and tell him that we're leaving and we'll meet him either at the *taverna* or on the coach.'

No sooner had Jack left her than Juliet stiffened, amazed to hear the voices of her aunt and cousin coming to her from behind one of the walls of the citadel. Where, then, was Dorian? she wondered, but this was soon explained.

'It was a pity that Dorian had to break his date with you, Tanya. He's having to supervise something on the yacht, you said?'

'That's right. He was terribly disappointed that he couldn't be with me.' A silence followed before her mother asked,

'Hasn't he said anything to you about *her?*'

'He never even mentions his wife, Mother.'

'It's easy to see that they've quarrelled, and seriously. She looks like a grasping little gold-digger to me, and it could just be that he's found her out, so he's finished with her. Dorian would be like that, you know.'

'A gold-digger,' mused Tanya, then added, 'But she'd be a little more clever than to give herself away on her honeymoon.'

'Then what is it that's made him neglect her in favour of you?'

'He was once madly in love with me, that's why. He's still in love with me.'

'But he didn't propose.' A silence followed; Juliet could almost hear her aunt's sigh of regret. 'Have you ever thought what a difference his money would have made to us at the present time? We'd have been able to leave the wretched Grange and get something more suited to our station in life.'

'You seem very sure that, as my husband, he'd have been generous enough to buy you and Father another home.'

'The Greeks are very parent-conscious, Tanya. Yes, Dorian would have seen to it that your father and I were resettled in a lovely country manor-house—or something with the same sort of prestige value.'

'If only I could persuade him to get rid of her!' Tanya's voice was harsh suddenly. 'He was mine before he was hers! Oh, if only he'd stayed at the Grange for a few more weeks! I'd have had that proposal from him—I know I would!'

'He's invited you to his home,' her mother reminded her. 'And that in itself is both revealing and promising. He's not in love with her, that goes without question, so you're in a most advantageous position. Play your cards right, Tanya, and before you know it he'll have divorced her and you will be his wife.'

Several times Juliet gasped, scarcely able to believe what she was hearing. So cool and calculating, those two! So confident the older woman that Tanya had only to play her cards right and she would soon become Dorian's wife.

'I can't understand why he married her,' Tanya was saying, and Juliet could see the thoughtful frown that was sure to be creasing her brow. 'She's beautiful—and there's no use pretending that she wouldn't have instantly attracted his notice. But for him to marry her....'

'You mean, it would have been more understandable if he'd just played around with her?'

'Seeing that they've already become tired of one another it certainly would have been better for Dorian. He's stuck with her now——'

'Rubbish! In Greece divorce is the easiest thing imaginable!'

'But they don't usually have divorces.'

'Dorian will,' was Mrs Lowther's confident assertion. 'And then you, my dear, will come into your own at last.'

'And come into the money. How fed up I am with scrimping and scraping the way we do!'

'It might not be for much longer, not if you're clever. You're still very beautiful, Tanya; and in addition you still appeal to Dorian, there can be no doubt about that.'

Looking up, Juliet saw Jack approaching, and she moved swiftly away from the wall.

'Ready, Juliet?' he asked, and she nodded her head. 'Come on, then, and we'll have that cool drink. I've told Leonard what we're doing and he said that as he's a lot of notes to take he'll see us on the coach.'

The *taverna* was found and the proprietor gave them a table right on the outside of the pavement. Jack shrugged and sat down resignedly. Juliet saw that he would have preferred somewhere less exposed to the stares of passers-by.

'Now that we're alone,' he said after the order was given, 'we can tell one another about ourselves. I'm a student at a college of education. What do you do for a living?'

'I'm married,' she said, and instantly saw his face fall.

'But your husband isn't with you?' He was staring at her beautiful face, quite plainly baffled that she was alone.

'He's gone off somewhere,' she told him casually. 'We're not the kind of people to be for ever under each other's heels.'

'But—' Bewilderedly he shook his head. 'If you're on holiday...?'

'We're on holiday, yes, but as I've said, we don't get in each other's way all the time.'

Jack regarded her with a troubled look.

'Are you happy?' he asked, just as if he had to.

Juliet laughed.

'Of course,' she said ... but what an untruth this was! She was dwelling on what she had overheard and the only picture that emerged from her mind was that of Tanya married to Dorian....

Jack was just about to speak again when Juliet was hailed—by Tanya.

'Hello,' she said, stopping by the table. 'I didn't know you were coming here today.' Her dark eyes settled curiously on the face of Juliet's companion.

'Did you come by coach?'

'Yes.'

'So did I. We could have come together.' She glanced round to where her mother was standing a short distance away, bargaining with a Greek woman who was selling hand-made lace traycloths. 'Perhaps we can join you? We're dying of thirst.'

Jack looked as if he had only just managed to hold back a scowl and Juliet had to smile at the relief on his face when she said,

'I'm afraid you can't, Tanya. We might be having someone else join us in a few moments.'

'Oh, I see.' Without another word Tanya turned on her heel and strode away to join her mother who, by this time, had managed to get the cloth at her own price.

'Friend of yours?' asked Jack as he followed Tanya with his eyes.

'No, not at all. She's staying at the same hotel as I, that's all.' No need to go into details with a stranger, she thought.

On arriving back at the hotel at half past six she saw that Tanya and her mother were in the lounge, talking to Dorian. Slipping past the open door, Juliet thought she had managed to reach the stairs unseen, but she had not been in the bedroom more than five minutes when her husband entered and Juliet looked frowningly at him, a question in her eyes. But he said nothing, merely standing with his back to the closed door, his gaze fixed most disconcertingly upon her.

'Is something wrong?' she inquired. 'You look ready to explode.'

The dark eyes glinted, dangerously.

'You've been out this afternoon,' he began, when

she interrupted to say,

'I've been to Lindos.'

'I know where you've been——'

'You do? Your friend Tanya told you, it would seem.'

'Do you mind keeping quiet! What I'm trying to ask is: who was the man you were with?'

'Ah ... Tanya again. Did you send her to spy on me or has she taken it on herself to do so?'

Dorian approached his wife, moving across the room as silent-footed as a tiger.

'I asked you a question,' he reminded her softly. 'Who was the man?'

She was tempted to hint that she had found a boyfriend, but reading her husband's expression she decided against it.

'He was someone I met on the coach; he sat next to me so we went up to the Acropolis together. There was another man with us, an older man.'

Dorian appeared to be satisfied with this, but warned her that she had better keep away from men in future.

'At least,' he added, 'until you and I part company. You can do what you like after that.'

'And you?' she inquired, seeing again her cousin married to him.

'That has nothing to do with you.'

'Tanya...?' The one word left her lips unbidden; he seemed to give a small start, after which he instantly lowered his eyelashes and said,

'Yes, Tanya!'

'You'll ... marry her?'

Dorian turned to look out of the window; Juliet could not decide whether his attention had been caught by something or whether he was deliberately avoiding her gaze.

'Probably,' he said at length, and once again Juliet found herself speaking impulsively.

'It's strange that you didn't marry her before.'

Without turning his head Dorian said quietly,

'It isn't too late to put right my mistake.'

'So—so—it was a mistake?' Within her something seemed to die; she fumbled round in her mind for an explanation of the way she was feeling. And the only thing that emerged was that she had once loved this dark Greek who was now her husband.... 'You w-wish you'd married Tanya—all that time ago?'

He turned his head at this, and as a slow frown began to form on his brow she did wonder if he had detected a catch of unhappiness in her voice. He examined her features with an intensity that strengthened this idea and at the same time disconcerted her. She lowered her head, avoiding that keen scrutiny. He spoke at last, in tones that held no expression at all.

'Yes,' he said, 'I do wish I'd married Tanya all that time ago.'

CHAPTER TEN

THE yacht sailed gracefully into the harbour at Thassos and Juliet breathed a sigh of relief. Very soon now she would be sailing away from the island again—this time sailing to freedom! Then Tanya, who had come to stay at the villa as Dorian's guest, could have everything all her own way—and good luck to her! Juliet had been infuriated by the way the two had practically ignored her on the entire homeward voyage, Tanya saying, in response to a protest from Juliet on hearing her cousin giving an order to Elias,

'If Dorian doesn't mind then why should you? You seem to forget that we're old friends, that I knew him years and years before you did.'

Juliet had turned away, aware that she would gain nothing by arguing with her cousin. After all, nothing mattered except the fact that escape was coming closer and closer with every mile covered. And now, as she stepped ashore, she glanced at the ferry that was anchored close by. Tomorrow she would be leaving on a similar boat.

Once at the villa, Juliet left her husband with Tanya and went up to her room. Restlessness mingled with urgency and she could have begun her packing right away. In fact, she did wander about the room, opening drawers and making a mental calculation of just how long it would take her to pack. Some things she meant to leave behind—the clothes which her husband had bought her, the shoes and handbags too. Her books she must take, she thought, her eyes falling to the shelf under the window-seat. Stooping, she picked out a book of poems which she had received for her birthday, a present from a colleague with whom she had worked. It had been bought from a secondhand shop, the suede binding and gold lettering having attracted the purchaser. Idly flicking through the pages, she recalled that Sunday morning when, after receiving Meg's lovely present of a silver-backed brush and comb set, she had quite literally related the story of her life to her friend. What a lot had happened since then! Her entire mode of living had undergone an upheaval, and all because of her desire for revenge. Juliet knew without an atom of doubt that she would go back if she could—undo all the damage she had done to her life by her thoughtless action in marrying the formidable Dorian Coralis.

Taking the book of poems with her, she went downstairs and into the sitting-room. It was empty and she sat down, impatient for tomorrow when this inaction could be replaced by a visit to the harbour to find out the time of the ferries, and to buy her ticket. She would have to time her departure very carefully, though, Dorian must not have the opportunity of stopping her from leaving.

She intended planting her suitcases in a little sheltered copse just along the road, a copse that could be approached through the gardens of the villa, along a very narrow path on both sides of which were thick bushes which would quite easily hide her from anyone looking out from the windows of the house. A taxi would be ordered to pull up by the copse, where she would be waiting.... Once aboard the ferry and she would be free!

How Dorian would fume when he realized that he had been duped! And he never would know whether or not he was a father....

Juliet looked up from her book as Tanya entered the room. The girl had been occupied with glamorizing herself—as she had so often been similarly occupied in the past—and she brought with her into the room a waft of heady perfume. Her hair was immaculate, her dress low and seductive, her crimson fingernails long and pointed.

'Oh ... I thought Dorian would be here.' With a swagger that the mistress of the place might just have used, she crossed the room and sat down. 'However, as we're alone we might as well talk.' Swinging one elegant leg over the other, Tanya looked arrogantly at the girl on the settee. 'Of course, you're looking surprised,' continued Tanya in a voice of unconcern. 'So I shall come straight to the point: just when are you and Dorian parting?'

'Parting——?' Juliet half rose from the couch, then sank back again. 'What are you talking about? Has Dorian told you that we're parting?'

A moment's hesitation and then,

'If I say yes, he has, what will your reaction be?'

'I shall go straight to him and complain——'

'I thought you would, so I'd better tell you the truth. That day when you'd been to Lindos, I happened to be passing your bedroom when you and Dorian were talking. He was asking about the man you were with, remember?'

Juliet, who had gone white with anger, felt the colour returning slowly to her cheeks. She nodded and said icily,

'I remember. You were listening, then—outside our bedroom?'

'Not deliberately——'

'I don't believe you, but do go on.'

The older girl's dark eyes narrowed.

'I heard my name spoken a few seconds after you and Dorian had been talking about the young man. I'd already heard Dorian say something about you and him parting company. Then I heard him say he would probably marry me—when you'd left him, of course.'

'Of course,' repeated Juliet, alive to the incredible fact that she was totally composed now—and ready for a fight! 'He could scarcely marry you while I was here—even the Greeks stop at polygamy.'

'There's no need for that kind of sarcasm!' snapped her cousin, anger bringing colour to her face. 'I might as well tell you that I heard quite sufficient for me to know that Dorian wants to marry *me*! I heard him tell you that he'd made a mistake in not marrying me a long while ago.'

'Well,' returned Juliet calmly, 'you might have heard sufficient for you to deduce that Dorian wishes to marry you, but now you're going to hear sufficient to convince you that marriage to him is not going to be possible.' Pausing, Juliet rather enjoyed the look of consternation that entered her cousin's eyes. 'You see, Tanya, I am not intending to leave my husband—not now or at any other time, so if you have any pride at all you'll pack up and leave my house!'

'Your house?' almost snarled Tanya. 'It will never be that! You'll have to leave—Dorian will make you! It's me he wants, *me*, I tell you!'

'I'm not arguing with you about that,' returned Juliet, picking up her book. 'I'm just passing on the information that if you're waiting to step into my shoes then you'll have to wait a very long time indeed.' She stood up, intending to leave the room, but the book slipped from her fingers and something shot from its pages, across to where Tanya was sitting. Stooping, she picked it up; Juliet saw her look at it, heard her gasp of incredulity before she said,

'Where did you get this?'

Frowning in puzzlement, Juliet crossed over to where her cousin sat and, extending a hand, she would have taken the small piece of pasteboard from her hand, but it was drawn back before she could even touch it.

'What...?' Juliet found herself staring down at a snapshot of Emily Lowther, a snapshot taken by Dorian over eight years ago. The last time Juliet had seen it was when she brought it from her box of private papers and had showed it to Meg. Juliet could not have said what happened to it after that; she assumed she had replaced it in the box. She now realized that either she or Meg had slipped it into the book of poems.

'This is a——' Tanya stopped, her dark eyes narrowed as they settled on her cousin's face. Juliet turned away; in a sort of desperation she endeavoured to regain her composure. What could she say? How could she get out of this? 'Where did you get it?' asked Tanya again.

Juliet gave a shrug, playing for time.

'Is it important?' she asked, still trying to collect herself sufficiently to be able to carry off this most dangerous situation with an air of unconcern. She was still so sure of her appearance being one hundred per cent deceptive that she was not unduly troubled about being recognized by her cousin. However, she had to give some explanation as to how the snapshot had got into her possession.

'Important?' Tanya's eyes seemed to bore into her for what seemed an eternity. 'Do you know who this is?'

Automatically Juliet shook her head; it was the only thing she could do. And then, right out of the blue, came the solution to her problem.

'A friend bought me this book; it was secondhand. She liked the suede binding and the gold lettering, so she bought it and gave it to me for a birthday present.'

Tanya's face fell. Juliet saw that although the girl did not know what she had expected, what she had received had disappointed her.

'This is a snapshot of my cousin,' she said at length, and handed it back to Juliet.

'Your cousin—Emily——?' Juliet stopped short as the door opened and her husband entered the room.

'Dorian,' said Tanya, gesturing to the snapshot which Juliet now held, 'do you remember taking a snap of Emily—it was in the garden at the Grange?'

Frowning in concentration, he at last said,

'Yes, I seem to recollect taking one.' He looked from Tanya's face to that of his wife, and then his eyes settled on the card she was holding. 'What's this all about?' he added in some perplexity.

'Juliet has that snapshot.'

'Juliet...?' His puzzlement increased. 'How can that be? Juliet didn't know her.'

His wife held out the snapshot, watching his face as he looked at it. He frowned—distastefully—and handed it back.

'It was in this book,' explained Juliet, avoiding his gaze. 'It was bought at a secondhand shop by a friend of mine who gave it to me for my birthday.'

'It was in the book? Let me have a look at the book.' A moment later he was saying, 'This wouldn't have belonged to Emily, would it?' He looked at Tanya, who instantly shook her head.

'I never saw it in her possession. In any case, she was hardly the girl to be able to appreciate this kind of poetry.'

'A very strange coincidence,' murmured Dorian

thoughtfully.

'Very strange,' agreed Tanya, and added, 'Juliet with this; Juliet with a voice similar to Emily's and hair the same colour. Juliet with the same name——'

'The same coloured hair,' interrupted Dorian. 'Emily had dark brown hair—in fact, it was almost black.'

Tanya was shaking her head.

'She dyed it. I thought I'd mentioned that Emily had hair the same colour as Juliet's.'

'Dyed it?' he repeated unbelievingly. 'No girl would dye hair that colour!' He was looking at his wife's glorious hair and shaking his head. 'I don't believe it.'

Tanya explained about Juliet's having seen the snapshot of Dorian.

'She fell in love with it,' she added, laughing. 'And as I had mentioned that you preferred brunettes to blondes she did no more than go out and buy herself a dye—just to make you notice her!' Tanya was still laughing and Juliet felt her cheeks start to burn. She expected some sort of disparaging comment from her husband and waited, prepared for more blood to rush into her face. But he staggered her when presently he did speak.

'She fell in love with my snapshot...?' He spoke softly, as if to himself. 'And so she dyed her hair ... just to make me notice her....' His mind was away, drifting into the distant past. His eyes suddenly shaded and when he spoke again there was a distinct edge of concern to his voice. 'I didn't know. I thought——' He stopped and a heavy frown knit his brow. Juliet watched him with a sort of fascination, seeing an altogether different side to his nature. Something stirred deep down within her; she too was in the past, walking in the woods with Dorian, thrilled to be with him, excited by his having consented to walk with her. She felt his kiss and with an automatic gesture she put a finger to her lips. He looked at her, attracted by the action of which she herself was unaware. But he did not see her; she realized this, for his eyes were vacant. He was still in the past.

'That child,' he was saying, and there was no mistaking the tones of genuine regret that edged his voice. 'I recall now, so vividly, that she puzzled me, but at the time I believed her to be....' His voice trailed away. He was unwilling to say more about the girl who had quite blatantly thrown herself at him. Could it be that he now realized that he had misjudged Emily Lowther? Juliet was sure that this was so.

'I don't think I understand you, Dorian,' Tanya put in rather impatiently. 'Emily was no good—you said so yourself——'

'I said your parents should watch her, yes, I admit it. But I didn't know then that she had fallen in love with the snapshot. You didn't mention this when I was condemning her.'

'What difference would it have made?'

'A great deal of difference, Tanya! I grossly misjudged that girl. And if there's anything I pride myself on it's being fair and just!' His anger was high, but it seemed not to have registered with Tanya, who pooh-poohed the idea that Dorian had misjudged her cousin.

'You ought to be seeing the funny side of it,' she pointed out, her eyes alight with amusement. 'A poor, ugly little wretch setting her cap at someone like you! Why, she wasn't fit to be your servant——'

'That's enough!' he snapped, and only then did Tanya grasp that he was furious. Her eyes flitted to Juliet, whose face was white and stiff, whose eyes were glinting with fury. 'We'll talk no more about the child!'

'Child—' pursued Tanya, lifting her eyebrows. 'She was no child! Old-headed and deep, more like. She deceived us, but we meted out ample punishment.'

Dorian's eyes were troubled as he asked,

'What sort of punishment?'

Tanya gave a resumé of what had happened, of how she and her parents had never allowed Emily to forget that she had almost brought trouble on to the people who had befriended her.

'We reminded her that she had acted in the most disgraceful manner possible. We let the entire village know, because we didn't think it right that she should be treated with any sort of respect whatsoever.'

Juliet, ignored in this interchange, stood very still, her mind in total chaos. She had told Tanya that she had no intention of leaving, but even while she said this she was accepting the possibility of Dorian's telling her to go—and this could be quite soon, since he could not be deceived much longer into thinking that she was expecting a child. In any event, Juliet had not even considered staying and her assertion to Tanya had been made in anger, and on the spur of the moment. But now.... What, she asked herself, had happened during the past few moments that had made her feel like this? —feel that she had lost the desire to 'escape' from her husband? Why was she upset because he was feeling guilty at misjudging Emily Lowther? Dorian was speaking now and she dragged her mind back, concentrating on what he said.

'The result of all this—er—punishment, as you call it?' Tanya's chin shot up; she had obviously taken offence at his words. 'It sounds more like persecution to me,' he supplemented, as if he would add fuel to the fire. 'Well, what was the result?'

Tanya hesitated; Juliet had to smile, for things were

not going the way her cousin had expected.

'She ran away.'

'Ran away....' Watching him as he repeated the two words, Juliet was staggered to see the sudden throbbing of a muscle in his throat, betraying an emotion that seemed altogether alien to the pagan traits which she had encountered in his nature. Without any doubt at all he was deeply touched by the plight of Emily Lowther. 'She went alone?'

'I expect she did——'

'But, earlier,' he interrupted harshly, 'you implied that she ran off with a man. That was a lie, wasn't it?'

Tanya frowned; sparing a sidelong glance for Juliet, she met only a stoical icy gaze. She licked her lips, hesitating uncertainly, and it was not difficult to see that she was almost lost for words.

'I don't understand what all this is about,' she complained at last. 'You were never concerned about Emily before.'

He eyed her with unutterable contempt.

'I didn't know everything. You mentioned in the hotel that you and your parents gave her love, dressed her in pretty clothes. I saw no pretty clothes, nor did I see any evidence of the love you mention.'

'I still don't understand.' Tanya spoke feebly now and Juliet wondered just how long she would stay here, taking all this from the man who, only a few minutes ago, was—according to Tanya—in love with her.

'If that book really was hers then she could be dead.'

'Dead?' Tanya looked at him. 'I don't see why you should say a thing like that.'

'Books that come into secondhand shops usually arrive there because their owner has died.' His mouth went tight, and that muscle throbbed in his throat again. Juliet's thoughts went rioting again as something stirred within her. For this man was so very far removed either from the Dorian Coralis she had first known, and who had caused her such misery, or from the arrogant and masterful husband who had without mercy bent her to his will. This was Dorian in his softest mood, the kind of mood she had witnessed when, at the beginning of their marriage, he had been so patient and loving with her, the man who had been so terribly hurt when she had told him that she had married him for his money, and not because she had loved him.

Her thoughts scattered once more and she was left with one only: she had once been in love with Dorian, deeply, madly in love. This one thought grew in importance as she stood there until, at last, she was admitting that she loved him still. Perhaps, she mused, she had always loved him, that the root had not perished, but had lain there, buried beneath the hatred that had been allowed to grow and flourish through the years. Yes, she loved him ... but she had thrown away her chance of happiness, for Dorian could never love her now; there had been far too much deceit, too much inflicted pain on her part, for him ever to forgive, let alone forget to the point where he could begin to care for her again. With a little trembling sigh she would have left the room, but Tanya's voice arrested her, as she commented on what Dorian had said about the possibility of Emily Lowther being dead.

'I don't suppose she is dead.'

'Then why have you never heard from her?' He glanced at Juliet as he said this, and she wondered if he were recalling that she herself had outspokenly told Tanya that some effort should have been made to find her cousin. Not that she had wanted any effort to be made—far from it! But she spoke as she did with the intention of bringing it home to Tanya that both she and her parents had shown an utter lack of concern at the disappearance of so young a girl.

'She doesn't care what's happened to us,' was Tanya's petulant reply.

Dorian was still troubled, and this was plainly betrayed by his expression. Juliet knew that his mind was occupied in looking more deeply into what had happened, and into the life which Emily had lived at the Grange. Older now than he was then, he could see more clearly and he must be owning that the little orphan child was nothing more than a slave to those who professed to have had her welfare at heart at the time they accepted responsibility for her. And because she was troubled by his self-condemnation Juliet smiled at him and said reassuringly,

'I shouldn't worry too much, Dorian. She'll be quite all right.' The softness of her tone, the anxiety in her eyes, the unconscious gesture of her hand ... all these affected him and, looking curiously at her, he asked,

'You sound concerned, Juliet.' She merely nodded and he went on, 'Is your concern for me ... for my peace of mind?'

'Yes, it is,' she replied quietly, profoundly aware of her cousin's glowering glance and the vicious tightness of her mouth. That she was furious at the way things were going was easy to see and it seemed to Juliet that she had decided to throw caution away, for she looked angrily at Dorian and said in sharp contemptuous tones,

'I don't know why any of us should be interested in the wretched girl! From the first she was a burden on us. And I expect she's now married to some labourer, and occupying her time rearing a brood of dull-witted children!'

Dorian stared at her, an exclamation rising to his lips, but it was Juliet who spoke first, spoke without a moment's thought, so uncontrolled was her fury on hearing these words of disparagement spoken by her cousin.

'She is *not* married to a labourer! Nor is she busy rearing a brood of dull-witted children!' Stepping closer to her cousin, she let her see the blazing fury in her eyes. Tanya, startled, moved back, but Juliet took another step towards her. 'How you hate and despise your cousin—how sure you are that she's made nothing of her life! The little slave, the girl you described as ugly, the orphan who had no say in the matter when her aunt and uncle decided to give her a home—*home*! A garret at the top of the house and the kitchen to work in! Such a girl couldn't possibly make anything of her life, could she?' Suddenly Juliet laughed in her cousin's face. 'But she did, Tanya. She found people who were human, and she made her home with them.'

She paused, vitally aware that her husband was staring at her so hard that his eyes were boring into her, eyes that examined and searched; bewildered, disbelieving eyes. Her first thought was that she had nothing to lose by a full revelation, since her marriage was at an end. Later, she would talk to Dorian, confessing that she had married him for revenge, confessing also that she was not expecting a child and never had been, that she had allowed him to believe she was, solely to gain her freedom at the earliest possible moment. He would not try to keep her—no, he would be only too willing to let her go. Would he let Tanya stay at the villa? Juliet doubted it . . . and the thought went some small way to easing the pain that was in her heart.

'It's obvious to you both that I am Emily,' she continued at length, her pensive eyes focused on the scene outside the window, the scene of tranquillity and peace, with the mountains and the sea, the sweeping lawns of the garden, the flowers and the shrubs, the little pool on which lilies floated in the sun. Peace.... It flowed over her all at once and her nerves were calmed. Dignity resulted; it enhanced the beauty of her features; it gave added height to her lovely slender body. She returned her attention to the two silent people in the room. 'After I left the Grange,' she said, 'I had an accident——'

'An accident?' It was Tanya who spoke; it was as if she found it impossible to remain quiet any longer. 'What sort of an accident?'

Juliet looked straight at her.

'I stepped under a bus.'

'A bus....' from Dorian and, sending him a sidelong glance, Juliet saw the depth of concern in his eyes.

'You see, Dorian, I had no money to speak of, and because I was thinking more of my immediate needs than of my safety, I unconsciously stepped off the footpath.' She went on to relate what had occurred from then on, relating it in exactly the same way that she had related it to Meg. The eyes of her companions interested her in their varied changes of expression as she progressed with her story. At last she terminated her narrative with, 'There isn't anything more that you don't know, Dorian. As for her——' Contemptuously she looked Tanya over, at the same time moving away, into the centre of the room, '——there's nothing more I want to say to her—except perhaps that I hope I shall never see either her or her parents again as long as I live.' Another glance at her husband and Juliet left the room, closing the door quietly behind her.

She had not been in her room more than a couple of

minutes when Dorian entered.

'Tanya's packing,' were his first words as he closed the door behind him. 'She'll be leaving by the nine o'clock ferry.'

Juliet, pale but composed, asked him why he was saying this to her.

'It's really none of my business,' she added, aware of the catch in her voice and hoping that Dorian had not heard it.

'It's very much your business, Juliet,' was his quiet rejoinder, and Juliet caught her breath at the edge of tenderness to his tone. Searching his face, she saw the little grey lines edging his mouth, the shadows that lay deep within his eyes. A dryness affected her tongue, but she managed to say,

'You mean—that you want me to stay with you?'

He seemed to swallow something that had lodged in his throat. He took a single step forward, then stopped.

'You loved me once——' He broke off, shaking his head. 'So much has been explained; I can see now why I was so puzzled by your behaviour—not only recently but all that long time ago.' He stopped again and looked at her. 'You married me for revenge, didn't you?'

'Yes, Dorian, I did.'

'I don't think I can blame you. I'd have done something similar myself had the positions been reversed.' She made no comment and he added, 'I'm glad it was for revenge, Juliet——'

'Glad?' she repeated, bewildered.

'Glad that it was revenge and not for my money. The money didn't mean a thing, did it?'

Without hesitation she shook her head.

'Your money had nothing at all to do with my reason for marrying you.'

'Tell me,' he said taking another step forward, 'has this desire for revenge been with you all those years?'

She did hesitate at this.

'My hatred for you lasted throughout the years,' she frankly owned. 'But I don't think the desire for revenge was there, simply, I suppose, because I never for one moment expected to have the opportunity of being revenged on you.'

Dorian became silent, and a long time passed. But eventually his reverie was broken by the piercing bray of a donkey on a nearby hillside and he spoke then, repeating what he had said already.

'You loved me once, Juliet.' A statement but a question as well; Juliet went forward, astounding herself by the ease with which she could say,

'I love you now, Dorian,' and the next second she was in his arms and his gentle tender lips had found hers in a kiss as passionate as it was reverent.

'My dearest wife,' he murmured, his cool breath fanning her cheek. 'What a fool I was, all that time ago, not to have seen that it was love you were offering.'

'Perhaps it was all for the best,' she said after he had kissed her again. 'The situation in which I found myself was such that it spurred me to make a move, to shake off the shackles. Had the situation been less intolerable, I'd probably have stayed on and on, never making a life of my own.'

'You're being generous, my love, and I don't deserve that you should be generous with me.'

Juliet merely pressed closer to him and lifted her face to his, debating on whether or not to make her final confession now or to wait until later. However, he both forestalled and startled her by saying,

'There isn't a baby, is there?'

'You know?' Leaning away, she stared at him. 'How?'

'I've only just made the guess,' he admitted, going on to say that it had dawned upon him that the deceit she practised could have been an act of desperation owing to his threat to keep her prisoner indefinitely. 'I've been a brute to you,' he added remorsefully. 'I don't know how you can forgive me, Juliet.'

At this near-humility she frowned, for she did not like it at all.

'But what of me—and the horrid way I've treated you? I wanted to hurt you, cruelly, and I think I succeeded. Never, *never* talk of what you've done to me, Dorian, because I've done much worse to you.'

'No, dear——'

'Oh, but yes——'

'Darling,' he cut in with mock-sternness, 'much as I love and adore you, I cannot allow you to argue with me. What I say goes, and life will be far more pleasant for you if you accept this.' But his eyes belied his tone, filled as they were with a wealth of tenderness not untinged with amusement. Juliet's eyes too were alight with humour as, adopting a meek and subdued manner, she responded with,

'I'll remember, dearest Dorian, and never argue with you again.'

He gave her a little playful shake, then drew her to his breast and held her in sweet and silent intimacy for a long moment before, holding her from him and looked gravely into her eyes, he said,

'Tanya ... she never meant anything to me. Can I convince you, Juliet?' So anxious his expression and troubled his voice. Juliet said,

'When we were in Rhodes, you paid her attention simply because you were—hurt?'

He nodded at this, and admitted that what she said was true.

'I invited her back here for the same reason, and because I wanted to humiliate you, to crush you——' He stopped abruptly and frowned. 'Darling,' he said presently, 'we'll not talk about such things again. I know that there are a few other trifles which we have not cleared up, but for the present——' He stopped again and gazed with tender emotion into her lovely eyes. 'For the present, my dearest, all I want to do is hold you and kiss you and tell you over and over again how much I love you.'

And as Juliet had no fault at all to find with this she nestled close against her husband and lifted her lips invitingly to his.